I0548807

Arctic Warriors

Ken Bangs

<u>Arctic Warriors</u> is dedicated to the Armed Forces of the United States of America.

Politicians set policy, Generals plan, but the cost of freedom is borne by the warrior.

Ken Bangs
Sergeant
Military Police Corps
Army of the United States

Arctic Warriors

List of Characters in <u>Arctic Warriors</u>

The Texans:
    Sergeant J.B. (Jacob Babb) Gideon – squad leader
    Rafer Torres
    Elmer Burtoff
    Eckie Wade
    Billy Gene (BG) Wilson
    Corporal Sonny Gritson (assistant squad leader)
    Gale Johnes (the shooter)

First Lieutenant Sam Groves - (Mission Coordinator)

Jake Tolbert – the traitor who defected with top-secret information

Layne / Nikita – Soviet spy working Jake for information

Demetrio – Layne's contact with Soviet intelligence in Fairbanks

Lieutenant Bosch – Charlie Battery fire control officer

Roscoe Mills – Military Police Sergeant escorting Jake from the fire control van

J.R. (John) Spalding – First Sergeant at Charlie Battery of the 562nd

Captain Ryan – Commanding officer of Charlie Battery of the 562nd

Luke Meek – Charge of Quarters (CQ) at Charlie Battery of the 562nd

Elias – Charge of Quarters at the 472nd who brought J.B. his orders

Archie Norwood – U.S. Army Criminal Investigation Agent at Ft. Wainwright who was killed by Nikita

Robert Dikes – U.S. Army Criminal Investigation Agent at Ft. Wainwright, killed by Nikita

Wilhelm & Janyke – Members of the Soviet Trade Delegation assigned to guard Jake when he defected

B.D. Fondren – U.S. Army Criminal Investigation Agent at Ft. Wainwright

Chief Warrant Officer (CWO4) John T. Johnson – Watch Command of the U.S. Army Criminal Investigations office at Ft. Wainwright

Greg Ransome – U.S. Army Criminal Investigations Agent at Ft. Wainwright
Scott Billings – Special Agent In Charge (SAC) Fairbanks office of the F.B.I.
Zack Mayfield – Special Agent of the Fairbanks office of the F.B.I.
David Box – Special Agent of the Fairbanks office of the F.B.I.
Colonel B. Ost – Commanding Officer of Ft. Wainwright Alaska
Sam Sorrensby – Special Agent for the U.S. National Security Agency
Jeanie Tallifore (real name Tasha)– A Soviet Intelligence Agent who had been able to join the U.S. Air Force as a Security Police officer and was assigned to the detention facility at Cheyenne Mountain
Officer Williams – U.S. Air force Security Police officer, assigned to the detention facility at Cheyenne Mountain
Officer Wheat – U.S. Air force Security Police officer, assigned to the detention facility at Cheyenne Mountain

Glossary of Terms Used in <u>Arctic Warriors</u>

CID - Criminal Investigation Division.

Claymore - An explosive weapon most often deployed as a mine, but can be adapted for different combat needs. It can be detonated by a trip wire or remotely.

Crossing Over - In <u>Arctic Warriors,</u> this is the practice of crossing the Bering Strait for military purposes on foreign soil.

Daisy Chain - The process of linking claymores together with detonation cord enabling employment simultaneously or in sequence.

DD - The "dd" in the sense of 'let's get the Hell out of here now!' comes from Vietnam era soldiers. In Vietnamese, "di-di mao" translates roughly to "get out" or "run!" The phrase got shortened to "di-di" over time.

DOD - Department of Defense.

EBR - Enhanced Battle Rifle as used in <u>Arctic Warriors</u> refers to a M14 rifle that has been modified for close combat. It is lighter, has a shorter barrel and is much more suitable for those teams in need of rapid movement.

Extraction - Removing troops from a given area.

Feet Dry - The point at which an aircraft is no longer over water.

Huey/Slick - Bell HU1 helicopter.

Incursion - The unauthorized entry of troops into the territory of a foreign nation.

Insertion - Placing troops into a given area.

KIA - Killed in action.

Klick - Kilometer or approximately two miles.

Lift Off - The point at which a helicopter becomes airborne.

LT - A Lieutenant, the commissioned rank above the enlisted rank of sergeant or warrant officer.

LZ – A designated place, landing zone, where a helicopter sets down to unload troops.

Mag – The storage unit from which ammunition is fed into the firing chamber of a weapon.

MP - Military Police. Often used to refer to a Military Police Officer.

MVD – The MVD is the ministry of internal affairs for the USSR, and today Russia. The troops of the MVD patrol the soviet borders.

M-14 - The standard issued 7.62 mm rifle for U.S. forces. It replaced the M-1 Garand 30.06 caliber rifle that was used by U.S. troops during WWII and Korea. It was replaced by the M-16 which became the standard issued rifle for U.S. troops during late 1967 early 1968.

Nike Herc - The MM1-14 Nike Hercules Missile used by the 562nd.

ORE - Officers review and evaluation.

SAC - Strategic Air Command best known for their operation the B-52 Bombers which during the height of the cold war were airborne around the clock armed with Nuclear bombs. The purpose was twofold; to ensure the ability to respond to any attack and to deter such an attack.

SAM - Surface to Air Missile refers to a missile launched from a non-airborne platform to interdict an airborne target.

Scope - The instrument displaying the flight path of a launched Missile. The missile's flight path and or destruction can be directed from a computer operated by the
fire control officer who is seated immediately next to the scope.

Scope Dope - The term used by MP's to refer to scope operators.

Scrote - Refers to the scrotum and is used to express disdain for an individual.

SDM - Squad designated marksman. In <u>Arctic Warriors,</u> this was Johnes who the team referred to as, Shooter. Johnes carried a different modification of the M14, one that had a scope, longer barrel, and the heavier 7.62 mm round needed for engaging the enemy at ranges out to 1,000 yards.

Shooter - The designated marksman (SDM) of a squad. Their primary assignment was to slow the advance of an enemy at long range and or to kill identifiable leadership in a firefight. In special operations squads, like the Texans in <u>Arctic Warriors</u>, these shooters were not detailed as snipers per se, but they would concentrate on a mission target who could not be captured alive.

Smoke - To shoot or kill.

Spook - Unidentified personnel thought to be spies or employees of United States Agencies generally associated with intelligence work.

Squad - Six soldiers and a sergeant.

STS - Surface to surface refers to a missile launched from non-airborne platform for the interdiction of another none airborne target.

Waste - To kill.

201 File - Personnel file of members of the armed forces.

562nd ADA - The five hundred and sixty-second air defense artillery battalion.

Contents

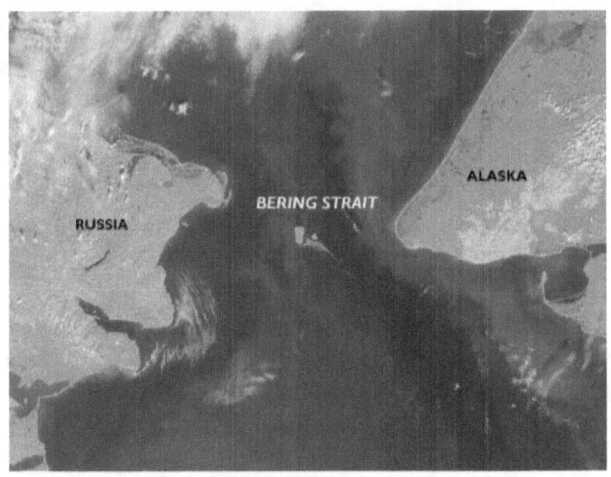

Prelude

The Bering Strait links the Arctic Ocean with the Bering Sea and separates Asia and North America. Its' depth ranges from ninety-eight to one hundred-sixty-four feet, and it is fifty-three miles wide at its' narrowest point. In winter, the region is subject to severe storms, and at times the sea is covered by ice fields four to five feet thick.

The international boundary between the United States (U.S.) and the Soviet Union (U.S.S.R.) runs through the middle of the Strait. Big Diomede and Little Diomede Islands are located in this passage. Big Diomede belongs to the Soviet Union and Little Diomede to the United States. At the closest point, two and one-half miles of open water separate the islands, thus the two greatest superpowers on earth.

This area has been a historical bridge for the peoples of the continents, Asia and North America, to cross from one to the other. The possibility of this bridge serving as an invasion route is obvious.

Crossing is possible by air, boat, or via the frozen sea with the ice bridge able to support light armored personnel carriers, jeeps and or trucks.

In an address to the United States Congress, in 1935, U.S. General Billy Mitchell is quoted as saying, "I believe that in the future, whoever holds Alaska will hold the world. I think it is the most important strategic place in the world."

The Japanese recognized the area's military importance and moved to gain control by invading the Aleutian Islands on June 3, 1942. They reasoned that control of the Aleutians would prevent a possible U.S. attack across the

Northern Pacific, provide them with a land base to launch airborne attacks against the U.S. mainland, especially the West Coast, and as a staging area from which to launch a land invasion of North America.

The U.S. and Canada were able to eject the invaders, but it took nearly a year and came with a loss of three thousand nine hundred and forty-two allied lives with best estimates of some five thousand Japanese killed in action. Never again has the Alaskan entry point been so lightly protected.

At the height of the cold war, the U.S. recognized the importance of blocking this invasion route and deployed naval, ground, and air defense commands throughout Alaska. The heart of the air defense was the Nike Hercules Missile used by the Five-Sixty-Second (562nd) Air Defense Artillery Battalion of the United States Army Alaska (USARAL). The 562nd had as its primary duty the protection of our Strategic Air Command (SAC) bases and the long-range bombers, carrying nuclear weapons and assuring a response to any attack from the Soviets.

Eielson Air Force Base was a SAC facility located approximately twenty-six miles outside of Fairbanks or some six hundred miles from our border with the U.S.S.R. The fighters and bombers stationed there served to check-mate any who would consider the Bering Strait as an invasion route, providing access to the continental U.S. and the deep- water ports along the West Coast. The 562nd defended Eielson with a ring of five Nike Hercules sites.

The missile sites of the 562nd were located in remote areas with the missiles themselves buried in hardened concrete silos deep underground. The formidableness of these nuclear birds made them a constant target for espionage. Security for the sites was a priority and entry was limited to those with top-secret clearances. Still, the chain is only as strong as its weakest link and, as often is the case, the weakest link was found within our ranks.

The Soviets directed their efforts to breaking through the chain of defense by infiltrating the military, and by employing traditional espionage tactics.

Military Police Officers, specially trained in tactics designed for the defense of nuclear weapons, were charged with the protection of these sites and the personnel assigned to them. Their focus was singular, to protect those atomic warheads. Their methods were aggressive.

Fairbanks was flooded with spies, often attractive women, who would prey on the lonely soldiers, gathering every scrap of information they could in an effort to create a breach in the chain of security protecting our most effective weapons systems.

The U.S. knew this, and engaged in counter-espionage efforts to ferret out the spies, and by deploying espionage agents to gather information on the Soviet installations so temptingly close. The result was conflict, a silent war that was ongoing, but, never acknowledged by either government.

The author was a member of the Military Police Group assigned to the protection of the 562nd. His novel, <u>Arctic Warriors</u>, is drawn from his arrest of a soldier who smuggled a camera into one of the silos and took photographs of a Nike Hercules missile.

The setting is Alaska, the time frame is 1968-69.

Chapter 1

The Storm

Turning to his team, J.B. signaled for them to stay put and maintain perimeter security while he moved out for a quick look-see. Pushing his way through the snow-covered brush, he made his way to the tree line and kneeled beside the trunk of an ancient Siberian pine.

He leaned his shoulder against the pine and raised his glasses to sweep the surface of the strait. The blowing snow filled the lens limiting his vision to the water's edge barely thirty yards away across the frozen beach. Lifting the glasses, he scanned upward with the same results. He saw nothing except the blowing snow that was beating a ferocious tattoo on his parka and mask covered face.

He dropped his glasses and slid around the tree, bracing his back against the trunk to maximize the shelter it offered. He knew his team was in serious trouble. This was supposed to be a quick in and out. *'Take the spooks in, let them set up their spy gear and then get out. This will take twenty-four hours, tops,'* the lieutenant had said.

At first, it did look easy. The insertion had been smooth. They had moved quickly and undetected to the point where the spooks wanted to place their equipment. The set up was accomplished quickly, and they moved to their extraction point on the beach. It was so simple, until the skies turned black and the arctic storm roared in dropping both temperature and visibility. Now here they sat, held captive by mother nature as sure as if they were locked in a Soviet prison.

'Focus,' J.B. told himself. *'Stop thinking about what you can't control and concentrate on that which you can. We are some twenty-six hours into this mission. That puts us two hours past our expected extraction time. We have food, two hundred and fifty rounds for each man, reasonably good shelter and we are undetected. So, we wait right here. This weather is keeping our bird from flying, but it will also keep the MVD from their routine sweeps along the water line. We should be good until the storm blows itself out and then for a couple of hours after that. We will stay under cover and there will be no tracks, no noise, and no images on their satellite.'*

Satisfied, J.B. leaned around the tree for one more look at the beach and then up into the skies. *'There is no change,'* he thought. Turning away he

14

moved carefully back to the shelter, dragging a branch behind him to erase his tracks. *'I probably don't need to do this. The new snow fall will cover them quickly,'* he mused.

Moving into the shelter, he called the team together and told them that they would sit tight until the storm blew itself out and then move closer to the beach, set up just inside the tree line and get ready for a quick sprint to the chopper.

He looked at the two spooks and said, "When I say go, I want you to fall in line behind my point man and run straight to the bird. Do not stop or turn back for any reason. If your partner falls, you keep going. We will take care of him. You get to that chopper, climb in, sit down and do not look back. Do you understand?"

The bearded men nodded but said nothing. J.B. turned to his team and said, "Spread out. I want you in a circle, five yards between each man with each man facing out. Your field of fire will be five yards either side of your position. We are going to sit still and remain quiet, we will not engage unless there is no other choice.

Set your weapons to semi-auto. Going full auto will burn too much ammunition. Choose your target carefully and try to stay in your fire zone. Do you have any questions?"

"What are you thinking boss? Are you guessing that our chopper will fly as soon as the storm lets up enough for it to be safe?" Wade asked.

"That is exactly what I'm thinking Eckie. They should be staged on Little Diomede; they will lift off veer east and come in fast and low.

We will be watching, and soon as we see them inbound, we will run for the water's edge. His flight in should take no more than ninety seconds. We will be there when the chopper hovers and slides the doors back. Three minutes more and we will be across the border and on our way home. Like the LT said, a piece of cake," J.B. smiled at his Texans.

As he talked J.B. became aware that it was no longer necessary to raise his voice, the roar of the wind had subsided. Looking up through the tree tops he saw the snow had slowed and the sky was beginning to turn from black to a dark blue.

The storm was dying as quickly as it had sprung to life. He looked around at his team and saw the smiles and the tension disappearing from their eyes.

"*Piece of Cake*," he repeated and led the team to the tree line.

Leaning against the big pine, J.B. lifted his glasses and swept the strait. *'There, is that our chopper? Yep, here she comes,'* he thought.

Without turning, he said, "The chopper is airborne. They have made the turn and are inbound to the beach. Form up. B.G., you have the point. Wait for my command and then move out at the double time."

"Roger that boss," B.G. said.

J.B. kept the glasses on the bird until he heard the first sound of the rotors. "Move out, B.G.," he said.

B.G. stepped from the tree line and started a steady jog toward the expected landing spot of the inbound chopper. The team followed, with Shooter at the six ,watching the woods. J.B. stayed as the rear guard until he saw the team reach the LZ, then he sprinted to join them.

The chopper came in at wave-top level. The pilot swung the Huey broadside to the beach, and the doors racked back. The gunner leaned out, covering the tree line with his fifty-caliber machine gun. Each member of the team stepped onto the runner and into the bird.

As soon as J.B. stepped in, the crew chief called, "Clear," to the pilot who had already pivoted and was out over the water as J.B. sat down. Three minutes later the chief looked at J.B. and said, "Welcome home."

J.B. nodded as the pilot flared the bird, and sat it down killing the engine. The doors slid back, and J.B. stepped from the chopper, followed by the spooks. Neither of the spooks looked at him or said anything. They simply walked away.

"This trip makes four times we have carried these guys across and brought them home safe. They don't carry any weapons, they don't carry any food or water, they never speak to us, hell they don't even acknowledge us. They simply get off the chopper and walk away without even a thank you. Who are they and why are we, a bunch of MP's, detailed to them?" B.G. asked.

"All I know is that they are connected with intelligence in some way. They do what they are trained to do, and we do what we are trained to do. We are all a part of a silent war. Leave it at that hoss," J.B. said.

Turning to the rest of his team he said, "Let's go debrief, and then get a hot

16

shower, a meal and some sack time."

"How long before we go again, boss?" Wade asked.

"I never know for sure, but I figure they will let us slide for a while.

Maybe, since we are all short-timers, this will be the last cross over," J.B. said.

"Right, and I have some beach front property in Nevada for sale," Wilson said as they turned and walked away to the debriefing.

Chapter 2

Hooked

Nikita rolled onto her back and lay staring at the ceiling. She was tired. The ever-present sun of the Alaskan summer filled her room, making it impossible for her to sleep.

She turned her back to the windows, and allowed her mind to wander. *'I hate Alaska, I hate America,'* she whispered.

Nikita hated America as fiercely as she loved her nation. She believed the Americans to be a collection of self-indulgent weaklings able to survive only because of their vast wealth and superb technology. That technology was responsible for their smart weapons, especially their missile defenses, which thus far had proven to be the equalizer between them and the mighty Russian Bear.

'If the Bearing Strait and then Alaska, are to be our primary invasion route into the North American continent, we must learn how to defeat these weapons and take their Strategic Air Command out of the equation. So here I am, working as a common whore to gather the information we need to take out the missiles protecting their bombers,' she sighed.

Her KGB contact in Fairbanks was Demetrio. He was a mongrelized Soviet from one of the Baltic States, and it annoyed her to have to accept instructions from him. But he outranked her in the service, so she obeyed him.

It was Demetrio who had installed her in the Polaris Club on First Street. He told her, "These soldiers soon grow tired of the native girls and come to the Polaris seeking the company of girls like those back home.

I want you to ply them with drink and use your sexual favors to draw them in, to keep them coming back to you. Concentrate on those assigned to the missile defenses and milk them for information."

That is how she had come to focus on Jake. Nikita noticed Jake staring at her as he sat in the lounge of the Polaris. She saw that he would sit for hours without taking a girl upstairs. She asked Sally, the receptionist, about him and learned that he had been a regular customer for about a year, and up until recently he would take girls upstairs.

Nikita pointed him out to Demetrio, and he followed Jake as he left the club. Demetrio told her, "He is the one we have been waiting for. His name is Jake Tolbert. He is assigned to Battery C of the 562nd Air Defense Artillery. He is from Iowa Park, Texas and his father is a well-known leader in their religious order.

He disgraced his family when he was arrested for soliciting an undercover policewoman, who he thought was a prostitute. The arrest caused quite a stir in his small hometown and threatened the promotion of his father to a teaching position in their order's seminary.

To remove himself as a distraction, Jake dropped out of school and joined the army. He was trained as an internal fire control specialist on the Nike Hercules missile and deployed to Alaska."

From that moment on, Jake was their target. Nikita made a point of positioning herself where Jake could see her as he entered the Polaris. She watched him as he remained aloof from the other soldiers and the staff. *'He considers himself to be an intellectual, cultured even, one who was different from the others who come in here,'* she decided.

She cultivated a persona to fit his self-image, and limited her interaction to those who were well mannered and gentlemanly in their approach to her. She knew he was watching her, *'The hook is baited and, he is circling the bait. Now ,I wait for Jake to bite,'* she mused.

Jake strolled into the Polaris and ordered a beer. He weaved his way through the crowd and sat at his favorite table. Here, he had an unobstructed view of the girl.

Jake sipped his beer and watched her. *'She is a whore, but she is different. She has a certain air, genteel even. And she carries herself in such a regal manner. I bet she has known wealth and privilege at some point in her life,'* he thought.

He watched her for a couple of weeks and noticed that she never approached a man. She sat waiting to be propositioned. He was impressed that she never went upstairs with the ruffians, only with those who were quiet, conducted themselves with some degree of dignity, and treated her with respect.

He was aware that she was avoiding him, not looking his way and he suspected that it was all part of a plan to attract his interest. He knew she was baiting him. But he could not help himself.

Jake was in love with her before he ever spoke to her. He knew her name was Layne; at least that was her working name. She was sitting on a couch, watching the sea of humanity passing by just outside the window when he decided to approach her.

"Good evening, Layne." His voice broke, and he stammered a little, but she looked up and smiled at him. Her eyes were a deep green. She wore very little makeup, and lip-gloss, but no lipstick. He was aware that she had said something in reply, but all he could hear was a roaring in his ears.

A haze settled over and around Layne. She sat in the middle of it, her beauty radiating out and washing over him in waves. Finally, she reached up, took his hand and pulled him into her world, guiding him down to sit beside her on her couch.

Layne knew Jake was struggling to regain his composure, so she sat holding his hand and looking into his eyes. Jake was breathless, drowning in her presence.

His lungs demanded air, and he gasped. Clarity returned as he sucked in a breath and his blood began to flow again. He had no idea how long he had sat staring at her.

"Are you okay, Jake?" she asked.

He nodded and asked, "How do you know my name?"

"I asked," she said.

"Why did you want to know my name?" he asked.

"You are different, such a gentleman. And, I am curious why you continue to come in here, but you never take any of the girls upstairs. Why is that Jake?"

"I used to take girls upstairs," he said. "But that was before I saw you. I don't look other women now. I have waited for you all of my life. You and me, we are meant for each other."

Layne said nothing. She withdrew her hand from his and lowered her eyes. After a couple of minutes of silence, she stood and picked up her purse. She paused, looked at Jake then turned to walk away.

Jake panicked and blurted out, "Layne, wait. Did I say something wrong?"

Layne stopped with her back to Jake then turned to face him and said, "I am a working girl. I like you, and had we met at another time, in another place, we might have had a personal relationship. But given my present circumstances, this is what I must do to earn my way, and any relationship we have will have to be based on an understanding of that."

"Sure, I get it. You like me, but you have to continue to work, right?" Jake answered.

"Exactly, and I can't afford to have any problems from a jealous man," Layne said.

"Okay, you won't have any problems with me," Jake said.

Layne gave him a long look and finally said, "Well, if you're sure you can handle the fact that I am a prostitute and you give me your word that there will be no issues with jealously, then I guess we can be friends."

"I'm sure. You have my word on it," Jake smiled.

"Okay then, how about buying my dinner big spender?" Layne laughed.

"You have a deal," Jake said. He took her arm, and they walked out the door. For the first time, Jake noticed that she was shorter than him. That was a new experience for him since he was only five feet eight inches tall.

Jake's heart soared as he bounced down the street with the woman of his dreams on his arm. *'And she is just my size!'*

Layne ordered a cheeseburger and a root beer, with fries and onion rings. She laughed when Jake said, "I thought you would want a sit-down meal with white table cloth and napkins."

"No, I am a West Texas girl. I like my burgers greasy, my root beer in a frosted mug, and Buddy Holly on the jukebox," Layne said, wrinkling her nose at Jake.

"Texas. I would never have guessed that. I don't hear the accent," Jake said.

"Well silly, where are you from? Texas, right? So, I sound like you. That's why you don't hear the accent," she offered.

"I guess that makes sense," Jake said, but he wasn't convinced. He heard something else, she was trying to sound like she was from Texas, but she was not making it. He sat thinking for a minute.

'Why would she lie about that? How does she know that I am from Texas?' Instinct told him to be careful, but love told him it didn't matter.

Dinner was great. They laughed and talked long after the burgers were gone. He played Buddy Holly's hit record, *Peggy Sue*, for her on the jukebox and she insisted they dance around the burger joint. The other patrons applauded them at the end.

He walked Layne back to the Polaris. She told him that she lived in one of the rooms upstairs. He said goodnight and turned to leave.

"Hey, you big dummy," Layne yelled and grabbed his arm. "I know I'm not ugly so it must be the onions on my breath."

"No, not at all. I didn't want to presume," Jake was saying when Layne cut him off in mid-sentence by grabbing his coat lapels and pulled him to her for a deep, lingering kiss.

"I had a great time, Jake. It is so good to be with a man who wants to be with me without, well you know," Layne said, as she looked up at him. "Please don't forget me."

She turned and ran back to the Polaris. The elegant, reserved woman had disappeared, and a vibrant young girl had taken her place. *'And she likes me,'* Jake thought. Jake had taken the bait. He was hooked.

Jake saw Layne as often as he could get a pass. Their relationship remained casual with long dinners and discussions on world events, philosophy, and religions.

"Tell me about your life Lane. Where are you from? How did you end up in Fairbanks; what did you do before?" Jake asked as they shared a root beer float at the A&W drive-in.

"I grew up in Lubbock. All of my family, on both sides, going back for generations have ranched in the area. After high-school, I went to Texas Tech where I studied to be a teacher.

I met a man named Roy Stewart. He was a pre-med major. We dated for the last three years of school and married a month after we graduated.

Roy was accepted to medical school at the University of Texas, Galveston branch. I taught school while he finished his medical degree. After medical school, we moved to Fort Worth where Roy completed his internship at John Peter Smith hospital. He was drafted immediately after finishing his internship.

The army commissioned him as a Captain and assigned him to Bassett Army Hospital at Fort Wainwright. That is how I came to be in Alaska."

"So, you were married? What happened?" Jake asked.

Lane sighed, looked out the window and asked, "Why is that important, Jake. Why are you asking all these questions?"

"I am trying to get to know you better. I'm wondering if there is a chance for us to become closer. To be more than friends," Jake said.

Lane paused thinking, '*He is suspicious. I am going to have to sleep with him and soon, or he will leave, and we will miss our best chance.*'

Her story was well rehearsed, and she decided to press on with it, "Okay, but understand something, Jake. I too have a say in the decision on whether or not our friendship becomes something more.
But for now, I will share this with you.

Our life was hectic. Roy was at the hospital a great deal of the time and I was teaching school in Fairbanks. But when we had time together, we had fun.

After about a year, I began to see a change in Roy. He seemed withdrawn, less affectionate and less interested in our physical relationship.

Then one day I was doing his laundry and saw stains in his underwear. I knew they were semen stains. I confronted him, and he had admitted that he was in love and having an affair with a fellow doctor at work.

I pressed him to tell who it was and finally, he said, '*You don't know him. His name is James.*'

I was devasted. We fought, and Roy moved out to live with James. I called the commander of the hospital and told him about Roy and James.

23

They were court-martialed and booted out of the army. Roy packed up and left Alaska, with his lover and without me. With Roy gone, I could no longer live on base.

The rumors and whispers finally caused the school to dismiss me. I was destitute with no job, no husband and no savings to speak of. So here I am nearly a year later, and still stuck in Fairbanks."

Jake sat watching while Lane spoke. She cried. *Or did she*? For the second time, he heard warning bells. *'I want to believe her, but I suspect she is lying.'* And for the second time, he disregarded the warning.

'She enchants me; or is it that I am lustful. Either way, I am hooked. She is beautiful, and she is the first woman who has ever really liked to spend time with me. She is worth any risk,' he decided.

Layne dabbed at her eyes and asked, "Jake, you don't seem to care about my troubles. Or, is it that you don't believe me? Why is it that when I let my guard down and open up with a man, the result is always the same? I get the feeling you are about to drop me, Jake. Is that it? Do I have too much baggage?"

"What?" Jake asked. "Don't be silly. I don't know what to say, I mean what can I say?"

"Well, how about saying, *I'm sorry Roy hurt you so much. Or, what a fool he was, wanting a man when he had you.* That would be nice to hear, Jake," Layne sniffed.

"Well, he was and is a fool. I mean that's so obvious it does not need to be said. Any real man would want to be with a beautiful woman, in an intimate relationship I mean, rather than another man," Jake replied.

"You're a real man, aren't you, Jake? But you don't act like you want to be with me. You have never tried to seduce me, Jake. Be truthful. Am I so unattractive that only those brutes at the Polaris want me?" Layne murmured.

"No, that is not the case at all. I mean, I do find you attractive," Jake paused.

"Do you find me attractive, Jake, or do you find me desirable?" Layne interrupted him.

Jake's throat suddenly tightened, so that when he tried to speak all that came out was a raspy croak.

Exasperated, Layne jumped up from the couch, grabbed Jake by the hand and led him to the elevator and up to her room.

Jake awoke with a start. "What time is it?" he asked.

Lane did not answer, and he rolled out of bed searching for his wristwatch. He found it on the dresser and saw that it was seven o'clock. He gathered his clothes from off the floor and dressed quickly.

He stumbled out of the Polaris and saw that the sun was well into its climb into the Eastern sky. He had to be back at Charlie Battery by eight o'clock. "This is going to be close. I hope my car starts," mumbled.

Jake ran across the street, jumped into the Chevy and turned the key. The battery was weak and labored to turn the engine over. But finally, the motor coughed and started. Jake sat waiting for the thick clouds of blue smoke to stop pouring from the exhaust, and for the engine to stop backfiring.

Once it was running smoothly, he shifted into gear, eased away from the curb and limped along until he could feel the power build and then pushed the accelerator down. He went speeding down First Street and turned onto the Richardson Highway.

It was a fifty-three-mile drive to Charlie Battery, and Jake had time to think about the night with Layne. Jake was no dummy. He knew that she had seen him drifting away and realized she had to set the hook that night. And set it she did!

'Now what? Layne is lying about her past. She is playing me, but to what end?' he wondered.

Jake sighed and inhaled deeply. Her lingering scent filled his senses, quickening his pulse and overcoming any thought of caution. 'Yep,' he thought, 'I am hooked, netted and landed.'

Layne was awake when she heard Jake ask what time it was. She pretended to be asleep as he bolted from her bed and started gathering his clothes from the floor. She fought to control her breathing hoping Jake would not see that Demetrio had been through his things during the night.

Demetrio was hiding in the closet when she and Jake entered her room the night before. He had a tiny camera and audio recorder mounted above her bed and used a small remote to activate them from his hiding place in the closet. He had a complete audio and video recording of their tryst.

After Jake fell asleep, she signaled Demetrio, and he crept out and pulled Jakes clothing into the closet. He photographed Jakes military identification card and made impressions of his dog tags.

Demetrio left the room to search Jake's car. Layne remained in the bed, ready to distract Jake should he awaken.

As soon as Jake rushed out of the room, she jumped from her bed and ran to the shower. She wept at the memory of having to let him touch her so intimately.

She stood under the scalding water scrubbing and re-scrubbing until her skin turned from a pleasant pink to a deep and irritated red.

Drained of emotion, she stopped the shower and stepped out to towel off. As she did, she renewed her resolve to bring this assignment to a quick end.

She wrapped the towel around her and sat on the side of her bed to call Demetrio. She allowed the phone to ring two times and then hung up and redialed. This time she let it ring three times and hung up.

She took a deep breath to compose herself and waited. The phone rang, and she heard Demetrio say, "Yes?"

"How long does this have to continue? I do not want to be a whore for the Americans. I cannot stand the thought of Jake touching me again," she asked.

"You know the deal. We must get the specifications and firing orders for the missiles. Jake works in the Internal Fire Control Van. He has what we need. You will continue to be his whore until you get what we need," Demetrio replied.

"We have him now! You filmed us last night. You have the audio of all he said. All we have to do is threaten to send copies to the Military Police. He will give us whatever we ask for," she pled.

"No. Listen to me, Nikita. We are not ready. You have to spend one more night with Jake. I will hide in the closet again.

I will film you having sex with him again. Do not be as passive as you were last time. You must convince him that you are in love with him. That is how you can get him to talk.

Ask him about his job. Tell him you are fascinated by missiles. Try to get him to tell you what type of missile he works with.

Ask him what he thinks about the military and his superiors. Ask him what they would say if they knew he was seeing the ex-wife of an officer. Get him to say anything that we can use against him.

When he is asleep, I will replace his dog tags and identification cards with counterfeits. If, when we confront him, Jake proves to be more resistant than we anticipate we will play the tapes for him and show him that we have his real card and tags. We will threaten to mail them to the military police with a note saying that we took them while he was having sex with a whore from Russia.

This will be over soon. Until then, remember you are Layne, not Nikita. Spread the net and catch this boy. It is for the motherland," Demetrio said and hung up.

She replaced the receiver and sat thinking, *'I have no choice. But once this assignment is over, I am asking to be transferred back to Moscow.'*

She stood and turned to walk into the bathroom. The phone rang, and she paused with one hand on the door frame. She looked back at the phone and thought, *'I hate that phone. Please, don't let it be a customer this early.'* Fighting down her disgust, she picked the phone up.

"Yes," she said.

"Honey, I know it is early, but we just had an oil field crew off of the north-slope come in, and we need all girls downstairs now." It was Sally, the front desk girl.

"That's okay, Sally. I'm getting dressed and will be there in just a minute," Nikita said.

She had hung the phone up and ran for the bathroom. She barely made it before the bile in her belly spewed from her mouth and nose. She retched until she was empty. She ran cold water over a cloth and wiped her face.

27

Settled as much as she could be, she walked from the room without rinsing her mouth or brushing her teeth. *'Nikita would never go to meet another with her breath smelling like this. But then, I will cease being Nikita the instant I walk from the room. The pigs I am going to meet will be drunk and not able to distinguish my breath from their own.'* Nikita opened the door, but it was Layne who walked from the room.

Chapter 3

The SOP Manual

Charlie Battery was hot. The general orders said that no personnel could leave the site during the week when their Battery was first in line to fire. The soldiers were also prohibited from making or receiving calls during this period. All calls into or out of the site were via the secure links, and were monitored and recorded.

Jake sat at the scope of the tracking radar in the internal fire control van and dreamed of Layne. He replayed their last night together over and over in his mind. He could feel her soft skin, smell of her hair, and the sweetness of her full firm lips. He sighed heavily.

"Are you okay, Jake?" He could hear the question but was not willing to leave his dreams of Layne to answer.

"Specialist Tolbert, get on your feet, and face me, soldier, right now," the voice commanded.

Jake turned to the sound of the voice and saw that it was coming from his duty officer. He looked around the fire control van and saw that everyone was staring at him.

"Did you hear me soldier?" the Lieutenant barked.

Jake jumped to his feet forgetting to unplug his headset. It jerked from his head and clattered to the floor of the van. "Yes, Sir?" Jake croaked.

"Where have you been Jake? I have been standing here the better part of three minutes now, and you never knew it. What if we had been in action?

You would have had no idea of where we were in the progression to fire. I need an explanation, and I need it now," the officer demanded.

"I'm so sorry, Lieutenant Bosch. I was daydreaming and didn't hear you. It won't happen again sir," Jake said.

"Your daydreaming could have killed our response to an enemy launch. Hell Jake, it could have delayed our response to the point that enemy birds

29

would have killed us before we could launch.

I can't risk having you in here. You are relieved. Step out and report to the Captain's office. Tell him I will be calling on the secure link to explain this event," Bosch ordered.

"But sir," Jake started to say.

"Are you still not hearing me, Jake?" the Lieutenant asked him.

"Yes sir, sorry sir," Jake stepped to the door of the van and punched in his code to unlock it. The door swung open, and the military police officer stationed there turned to look at Jake and the duty officer.

"Sign him out and escort him to the Captain. He is not to leave the site. Notify his relief that I need him here ASAP," Bosch said.

"Yes sir," the M.P. replied. He took Jake by the arm and walked him to the desk where the logbook was located. He pointed to the log and said to Jake, "You know the drill. Fill in the blanks with your name, rank, serial number, time out, and the reason for leaving. In this case, put *relieved by Lieutenant Bosch.*"

"No need to be so harsh, Roscoe," Jake said to the M.P. sergeant.

"Specialist Tolbert, you will refer to me as Sergeant Mills, and you will do as I tell you. Do you understand?" the sergeant asked.

Jake sighed, nodded, and signed out as instructed. As he turned to leave the secure area, Jake realized that he still had his copy of the internal fire control standard operating procedures (SOP). Part of his responsibility in the van was to maintain physical control of the SOP in the event they were ordered to fire on an enemy or in case the Lieutenant needed it in an instant.

The SOP Manual contained the firing order for all five batteries and the activation code necessary to begin the first phase of preparing the birds for flight.

Jake had punched a hole in the vinyl cover, looped a fine beaded chain through it and then hooked it onto his belt with a metal clasp. The manual was there, secured to his belt when he exited the internal fire control van.

Jake had been so upset with the events of the morning that he had forgotten it and no one else had noticed it either. Jake supposed they had seen his hands empty and just never thought about the book; or were so used to seeing it dangling at his side that its' presence had failed to raise an alarm.

Possessing the SOP manual outside of the fire control van was a breach of security procedures, but taking the top-secret document outside of the fire control area would be a felony.

As they approached the doors, Jake saw his field jacket hanging on the coat rack. He took the coat off the hook. He paused and shrugged into the coat as the M.P. opened the door.

The jacket was a three-quarter length, so it hung over and covered the dangling notebook.

As they started through the doors, Jake knew he should say *'wait a minute,'* and take the manual back to the door of the van and accept the consequences of his breach of security. In that instant, he heard his fathers' voice, *"Son, nothing ever remains hidden. The good book says that you can whisper something in a closed room and in the end, it will be shouted from the rooftops. It is always best to fess up and take your medicine."*

Jake knew his father was right, but he stepped through the doors and out of the secure area with the manual concealed under his field jacket. He was now committed to getting the book back inside before anyone noticed that it was missing. And he knew that until he could get it back inside, the book had to stay in his possession. *'But how was he going to do that without getting caught with it,'* Jake wondered.

"Come on Jake, no use lagging. My orders are to deliver you to Captain Ryan, and that's where you're going," Sergeant Mills said.

Jake stepped up beside the sergeant and into the Captain's reception area. First Sergeant John R. Spalding looked up with a scowl on his face. "What do you want," he growled.

Mills replied, "Lieutenant Bosch told me to bring Jake to the Captain."

"What the hell for?" Spalding barked.

"I don't know Top. Maybe Jake can tell you," Mills replied.

"What's this about Jake," Spalding asked.

"I messed up, Top. The lieutenant told me to report here and tell you that he would be calling the Captain on the secure link," Jake said.

"He said he was going to call on the secure link? Hell boy, we're hot. He knows better than that, unless it is for a mission critical event. Jake, what the hell did you do that would prevent us from fulfilling our mission?" Spalding asked.

"Well, it's like this, top. I meet a girl in Fairbanks a while back. We have become pretty friendly, and well I was thinking about her and missed the Lieutenant's progression on the half-hour squib tests," Jake stammered.

"Just exactly where did you meet this girl, Jake? Was it at the Polaris by chance?" Spalding asked.

Jake felt his face flush hot as the blood rushed to it. He nodded his head yes.

"Boy, don't shake your head at me. You answer me and damn it, Jake, I want you to stand up straight and look me in the eye. Do you understand me?" the First Sergeant rasped.

Jake snapped to attention and looked up at his First Sergeant.

"What do you know about this whore, Jake?" Spalding asked.

"She's not a whore, Top," Jake said.

"The hell you say. Didn't you tell me you met her at the Polaris?" Spalding asked.

Jake nodded and then seeing Spalding's face, he quickly said, "Yes, Top, that is what I said. But she's not like the rest of the girls there. I mean she does turn tricks, I know that but..."Jake stammered as his voice trailed off.

"Well now Jake, I can see that you've fallen for this whore. And let me tell you, Jake, she is a whore. You're not the first to be far from home and fall for some pretty face, and soft voice with *a marry me and take me away from all of this tale.*" He paused.

"Sergeant Mills, Jake is not to leave this office," Spalding said.

The MP Sergeant stepped over in front of the only exit and said, "Sit down Jake. You are not going anywhere." Jake shrugged, shoved his hands in his pockets and slumped down into a chair.

Spalding knocked on the Captain's office door. There was no answer. Spalding knocked again and said, "Sir, we got an event out here, and it looks like it is going to be mission critical sir."

The door swung open, and Captain Ryan said, "Mission critical, how so?"

"Sir, Lieutenant Bosch is duty officer in the van. He has relieved Specialist Tolbert and remanded him to the custody of the military police, to be escorted to you. The specialist reports the Lieutenant instructed him to inform you that he would be calling on the secure link to explain sir," Spalding said.

"No! Get a runner to the van and tell him to stay off of that link. Wake up the second shift duty officer and have him relieve Bosch. Tell Bosch to report here ASAP," Ryan ordered and walked back into his office closing the door in Spalding's face.

"Yes sir," Spalding replied to the closed door. Spalding walked to his desk, picked his phone, and spoke into it, "Get the charge of quarters to my office on the double."

He hung up and leaned back in his chair looking at Jake and Mills. He turned his head and looked at the calendar hanging on the wall beside his desk and said, "Forty-one more days and I won't have to deal with this anymore. Thirty-five years is enough."

"You want me, First Sergeant," Luke said as he slid in through the door.

Spalding looked at him with disdain. "Sergeant Meek, how many times have I told you that I do not want you sliding on my polished floors? Maybe I need to let you strip, wax and buff them to get the point across," Spalding said.

The smile left Luke's face as he said, "Come on, Top. I'm a buck sergeant. You can't have the troops see your sergeants doing manual labor."

"That's easy enough," Spalding said. "I made you a sergeant, and I can unmake you, just as quickly. Are we clear on this, troop?"

"We are clear, Top," Luke said.

"Good. Now get upstairs, and wake the second shift duty officer. Tell him Captain Ryan said for him to report to the van on the double and relieve Lieutenant Bosch," Spalding ordered.

33

Luke turned to leave and Spalding stopped him, "Luke. Remember you are talking with an officer, but tell him not to take time to pee, wash his face, or brush his teeth. He should be dressed, so all he needs to do is get his boots on, and hustle downstairs to the van."

"Got it, Top," Luke said as he dashed out the door and ran for the stairs.

Five minutes later, Lieutenant Bosch walked into the office. Spalding stood and said, "This way, sir. The Captain said to bring you right in."

Spalding knocked once and opened the door. Bosch walked in and closed the door behind him.

After a few minutes the intercom on Spalding's desk beeped, and he walked into the Captain's office.

"John, what's going on with this kid? Does he realize we could have lost the SAC base in a live fire situation?" Ryan asked.

"Sir, I don't know what he realizes; but what's going on with him is that he has fallen in love with a whore from the Polaris. My guess she is his first love and he was sitting there daydreaming about her. He told me he was so far gone that he didn't hear you speaking at all, Lieutenant," Spalding said glancing at the duty officer.

"What do you think First Sergeant? Is this serious enough threat to involve the DOD or should we report this gal to the CID and let them find out about her?" Ryan asked.

Spalding rubbed his burr cut head and sighed. "You know boss, if I had to guess this is just a whore thinking she has latched onto a kid so green she can milk him dry or maybe even get him to marry her and take her away from the Polaris. But on the other hand, if she is a commie agent and she has worked him for information, then yes sir we could have a serious breach of national security here."

"Lieutenant Bosch, Jake is your man how well do you know him?" Ryan asked.

"He is the best scope man we have. Jake knows the fire control process so well that he can do any of the jobs, and that includes mine. He's close to being brilliant and assumes the lead on whatever shift he is working," Bosch said pausing.

34

Ryan sensed Bosch had something else to say, "Go ahead, Lieutenant."

"Well Sir, Do I think that a girl paying him attention could pull Jake off track? Yes, sir, it could happen. Does he have information about the internal fire control operation that could prove useful to a foreign agent? He does, sir.

Jake has worked for all the duty officers so long that he reads their mind. It's not uncommon for him to finish a step before they have given the order. He has mastered their tendencies, and that includes their random selection of firing codes," Bosch reported.

The captain sat chewing on his bottom lip. He thought about the results of reporting this to the DOD. Agents would flood his command, and the interviews and investigation would go far beyond Jake and this one incident. He also thought about how it would reflect on him as the battery commander and what impact it would have on his next review and evaluation.

His mind made up, Ryan spoke, "As of this instant I am declaring this to be a classified incident. I'm not yet willing to call it a mission critical event.

Sergeant Spalding, you will contact the Military Police Criminal Investigation Division at Fort Wainwright and brief them on this incident. You will stress to them that I have declared this to be a classified but not mission critical incident. You will convey to them that as Battery Commander I am reserving oversight and disposition authority pending their report to me concerning this girl. I want that report to include their assessment of her as a threat to national security and our mission. Do you have any questions, First Sergeant?"

Spalding said, "No Sir."

"Good. I want an answer on my desk eight days from now. That gives the agents seven days to complete their investigation and write their report. It gives you, First Sergeant, one day to review and revise it before the final draft is given to me." Ryan stood to signal the meeting was over.

"Sir, what do you want to do about Jake while we gather the information on this girl?" Spalding asked.

"Jake is your man, so that makes it your call, First Sergeant. Just be sure he does not have access to any secure areas," Ryan replied.

35

Bosch and Spalding walked out of the Captain's office and closed the door. Bosch asked, "Do you need anything from me, First Sergeant?"

Spalding replied, "Not unless you can make this go away sir."

Bosch laughed and said, "If only I could."

Spalding said, "Jake, I want your military Identification card, your dog tags, and your pass. You are restricted to quarters.

You will not discuss this incident with anyone except with my knowledge and approval. You are not to enter into any area requiring a clearance. I'm telling you Jake, and you had better listen to me, violate any part of what I just told you and you're headed to Fort Leavenworth just as sure as God made those little green apples."

Jake handed over the items Spalding had asked for. Spalding said, "Okay, Son. Now, go upstairs to your quarters and get some rest."

Spalding turned to walk away, and Jake just stood there. Spalding stopped and turned back to face Jake. He stared at Jake, leaned forward and said, "Jake, I see something in your eyes that worries me. Do you have something you want to get off your chest, Son? Now might be the best time."

Jake gulped. He knew that the SOP Manual hanging on his waist was pulling him down into a dark hole from which he would never be able to escape. He opened his mouth to speak, but instead of telling Spalding about the manual he heard himself saying, "No Top, I guess not."

Jake walked out of the office and climbed the stairs to his quarters. The manual swinging against his leg reminded him that with each step he was walking deeper and deeper into the dark recesses of a military prison. Yet, he walked on.

Jake hid the manual under his mattress where he could feel it as he lay on the cot. It was comforting to know where it was and at the same time a constant reminder of the problems it represented.

'Each scope operator has a copy of the manual. Mine may not be missed. If I can get a quick return to duty, I will walk back into the van with the manual covered by my field jacket. Once inside the van, I will sit in the chair and take the coat off. The manual will be hanging from my belt, just like always. No one will know that I took it outside the van,' Jake ran the plan through in his

mind.

Jake thought a lot about Layne. He knew there was something she was not telling him, and he knew her Texas accent was a fake. He also suspected she was lying about her husband and his dismissal from military service. *'None of her story made any sense. A quick call home and her family would have sprung for the ticket out of Alaska,'* he reasoned.

But man, she was fine. His thoughts always wandered back to their last night together, and he would pace the floor in anticipation of seeing her again.

————————————

On Wednesday two CID agents came to his quarters to interview him. They had his personnel file and didn't ask much about his military service. They did, however, ask a lot of questions about Layne. Jake was frank with them. He told them all his suspicions about her and volunteered that they had been intimate.

The lead investigator was named Archie Norwood. "We appreciate your being upfront with us. Has she questioned you about your job here at Charlie Battery?" he asked.

Jake was relieved that he was able to speak truthfully when he said, "Not at all. No questions and nothing to do with me being a soldier, except for her asking me how I could afford to court her on my army pay."

"What was that about?" Agent Norwood asked.

Jake grinned sheepishly, "I always take her some small gift when I go to see her. Nothing big, I don't have much money. She considers the giving of gifts or buying a meal as courting."

"If there is anything else you want to tell us, now is the time. It will best for you to clear all of this up right now. Don't leave any door open so something can come through and bite you in the butt. Let's get it settled now," Norwood said.

Jake thought a minute. He considered telling them about the manual but swallowed and said, "No, not really. I know Layne is playing me, but I'm playing her too. I have three months left on this tour, and then I will rotate out of here, and she will be history. In the meantime, I get lonely. Know what I mean?"

Norwood nodded. "Yep, I am here alone too. But let me get off that and tell you this, Jake. I have been doing this for a while now. I have learned to read men pretty well.

I just saw something in your face, a tightening around the eyes that lets me know that you were thinking about telling us something. Then you swallowed, and moved on.

Don't let us walk out of here with something left unsaid. Once we go through that door, you are going to be left standing on what you have told us. There will be no mercy from that point on. Do you understand?"

Jake stood, extended his hand and said, "That's it, guys. I am looking forward to getting this all behind me so I can get back to town and see Layne."

The agents looked at each other and walked out leaving the door open. At the end of the hall, they turned and looked back to where Jake stood watching them. Jake waved, and walked back into his room.

Deep down inside Jake knew his last chance to come out of this with some hope of a future was disappearing with the echo of those footsteps growing ever fainter.

He stopped by the First Sergeant's office after chow later that day. Spalding did not want to talk with him but did tell him they should have an answer by the end of the week. That was two days away. Maybe he could get his pass back and head to Fairbanks.

Jake lay down at noon on Friday hoping to sleep through the rest of the afternoon or until his news came. He had just drifted off when the door swung open.

"Get out of that bunk, Jake. Top said to get you to the Captain," Sergeant Mills said.

"So, why you and not the Charge of Quarters?" Jake asked as he pulled on his boots and zipped them up.

Mills didn't answer. Instead, he raised his baton and pointed down the hall toward the stairs with it. His intent was clear. Jake trotted out of the room and headed for the stairs.

"Stop it, Jake. There is no need to run," Mills scolded.

Jake walked into Spalding's office. The First Sergeant rose and pointed to the open door of the Captain's office.

Jake walked to the door, knocked, and heard the Captain say, "Enter."

Jake strode to the front of the Captain's desk, saluted and said, "Specialist Tolbert reporting as ordered sir."

"Stand at ease Specialist," the Captain said after returning Jake's salute.

"Jake, I want you to realize just how close you have come to spending a couple of years in jail," Captain Ryan began.

Jake knew the Captain was still speaking, but those first words allowed relief to flood his whole being. He knew that he was going to lose some skin, but he had survived the investigation.

"You have been playing the fool with this little whore, but the CID tells me that you know what she is and that you are playing her just as much as she is playing you. And, you were right in what you told the agents about her. That story about her husband is all bogus. She has spent some time in Texas, but that was just another stop along her way.

They are recommending a full DOD investigation to determine who she is and where she is from. But that would involve the FBI as well, and I am not convinced this is any more than a whore trying to find a ticket out of town. Therefore, I am exercising command authority and ending the investigation," Ryan paused and then continued.

"I have agreed, out of an abundance of caution, to suspend your clearance. I am also going to reduce you from Specialist Six to Specialist Five. You have three months left on your tour here in the Alaskan Command. You will spend the remainder of your tour on a permanent charge of quarter's duty. You will work five days on and two off. Do you have any questions or comments, Jake?"

"No sir I don't have any comments except to say thank you, sir. But I would like to know if I get my pass back," Jake asked.

Ryan leaned back in his chair and said, "That's all? Can I get my pass back sir? Hell Jake, you're just like that moth. Headed right back to the flame, aren't you?"

Jake didn't respond.

"Sergeant Spalding, come in here please," the Captain called.

"Sir?" Spalding stood before the desk alongside Jake.

"You know my decision. Give him my written orders reducing his rank by one grade, put him on permanent C.Q. and pull his clearance. Give him his pass, dog tags, and identification card."

"Yes sir, is that all, sir?" Spalding asked.

"Yes, that is all," the commander said.

Spalding walked to his desk and handed Jake the orders reducing his rank and withdrawing his clearance. He then opened the safe and gave Jake his dog tags, his pass, and his identification card.

"I know you will not listen to me Jake, but my advice is that you sit right here on this site until you catch that freedom bird back to the world," Spalding said.

"Can I go, First Sergeant," Jake asked.

Spalding nodded his head.

Jake turned on his heel and walked out . By the time he had reached the stairs, he was running.

He pounded up them two at a time. It was Friday, Layne was in Fairbanks, and he was burning time.

Chapter 4

Enemy of The State

Layne was sitting on the couch in the front room of the Polaris and saw Jake as he parked on First Street. She moved quickly to the elevator, wanting to get to her room so she could call Demetrio before having to face Jake.

She grabbed her phone and dialed Demetrio. The phone was picked up, but as expected there was silence. "He's here now," she said. The connection was broken, and the dial tone came on.

Layne hung the phone up, and there was a knock on her door. She smoothed her dress, took a quick look in the mirror, and stepped to the door. "Yes?" she called.

"It's me," Jake said.

Layne opened the door and threw her arms around him. She pushed up on her tiptoes and kissed him on the lips.

"Wow," Jake gasped when Layne broke the kiss. "I've missed you too."

Jake sat the backpack he was carrying down beside the door, closed the door, and reached for Layne. Putting his arms around her, he kissed her again and moved her backward to the bed.

She pushed him away and said, "Slow down, Jake."

Jake had already pulled his shirt over his head and had one leg out of his pants when the door burst open. Demetrio crossed the room in one stride and slapped Jake with a huge right hand.

The force of the open-handed blow dropped Jake onto the bed. Demetrio pulled the dazed Jake off the bed and slapped him again. Layne closed and locked the door.

"You American pig. You will never touch her again," Demetrio hissed.

Jake wiped the blood from his mouth and looked at Layne. She said, "I detest you, Jake Tolbert."

"What is this?" Jake asked.

"This, Jake Tolbert of Iowa Park, Texas, is where you pay for the pleasure you have taken with Nikita," Demetrio said.

"Why did he call you Nikita? How do you know where I am from?" Jake looked from one to the other.

"Shut your filthy mouth. Don't even say her name," Demetrio stepped toward Jake.

"Okay, don't hit me," Jake whimpered. "What do you want from me? Money, is this a shakedown? I don't have much, but my wallet is there in my pack, and you can have it all. Here, take my car keys too. I parked across the street."

Demetrio looked at the pack Jake had left by the door. He picked it up, sat it on the bed and opened it. He saw something that looked like a notebook and pulled it from the pack.

Jake jumped forward saying, "No, not that. You cannot have that."

Demetrio hit Jake in the chest with a closed fist. Jake collapsed, gasping for breath. Demetrio looked at the book, opened it and smiled.

"As the Americans say, *bingo*. We have hit the jackpot," he laughed.

"What is that?" Nikita asked.

"It is more than we could have hoped for. It is the Standard Operating Procedures, along with the technical specifications of the Nike Hercules missile. It has the firing order, the alternative sites, the arming and launching codes for all of the Battery Sites of the 562nd Air Defense Artillery located in this theater of operations," Demetrio said as he thumbed through the manual.

"You fool," he said as he looked at Jake. "You stupid fool. Why would you have this outside of your duty site?"

"I wanted to keep it safe," Jake whispered.

"What does it mean, Demetrio?" Nikita asked.

"It means we don't have to work this idiot. We have gained all we need because of his stupidity," Demetrio answered.

"Now what?" she asked.

"Gather your things. We are leaving now, immediately. We must get this manual to our people."

"What about him?" Nikita asked.

"You get your things, take his keys and wait for me in the car. I will tie him up and meet you there in a couple of minutes," Demetrio told her.

"You are going to leave him alive? Is that wise?" She asked.

"Nikita, allowing him to live will ensure that we will never have to come back to the West. If we kill him, he will not be able to tell them about us. If we leave him alive, they will get everything from him. Our names and our faces will be in their databases and we will never be sent back to America."

Nikita grabbed her bag and started to pack. She stopped and laughed. "What am I doing? I want nothing to remind me of this time, of this place. I am leaving it all."

She picked up Jake's keys and walked to the door. She unlocked it, paused with her hand on the knob and looked back at Jake. As she started to speak ,the door was thrust open. She was propelled across the room and crashed into Demetrio. She and Demetrio lay in a tangled heap on the foot of her bed.

"Show me your hands, now!" Nikita heard a male voice say.

Rough hands pulled her to her feet, spun her around, and pushed her against the wall. She looked over her shoulder to see a big man with a pistol held against Demetrio's right ear.

"Close the door, Robert," the big man said.

The second man in the room closed and locked the door. He then said, "My name is Robert Dikes. This is my partner Archie Norwood. We are special agents with the United States Army.

We have been standing outside, and heard everything you said. We are placing all three of you under arrest for violation of the Espionage Act."

Agent Norwood said to Demetrio, "I am going to step away from you. You will notice that I still have this pistol pointed directly at your head. Any act of resistance or aggression on your part, and I will shoot you. Do you understand?"

Demetrio nodded his head. Norwood said, "Stand and face the wall behind the bed. Place your hands on the wall and spread your feet."

Demetrio did as he was told, and Agent Dikes placed handcuffs on him. He then moved over to Nikita, put one hand on her shoulder and pulled her away from the wall.

He held his hand out, and Norwood placed a set of handcuffs in his open palm. Dikes snapped them on her wrists and stepped away.

"What about Jake?" Norwood asked.

Dikes replied, "I am out of handcuffs boss. But of the three, he is the one who will give us the least trouble. It is, what it is."

Norwood holstered his weapon, pointed his finger at Jake and said, "Jake, you had a chance to help yourself, but you just couldn't stay away from her, could you?"

Dikes nodded at the notebook lying on the floor. "What's that Jake?" he asked.

"I think it's best if I don't say anything. I want a lawyer," Jake said.

Demetrio laughed. "Idiot," he said. "Do you think you will ever see a lawyer, or a courtroom for that matter? You are more than a traitor, more than an enemy of the state.

You, little man, are an embarrassment, proof that the vaunted United States Army cannot secure their weapons or control their personnel. You will disappear, along with us, into some military prison."

While Demetrio was speaking, Norwood picked up the manual. He looked at the first page and whistled. "You were right, Robert. He was hiding something from us. This is the SOP Manual for the fire control operations at a Nike Hercules site."

"Please, I must use the restroom," Nikita said.

"Not a chance, little lady. Those handcuffs are not coming off, and you are not getting out of our sight," Dikes said.

"What are you thinking, Archie?" Dikes asked Norwood.

Norwood looked at the telephone beside the bed. "It does not take all day to look at a horseshoe. This is a now a National Security Issue.

We have the SOP Manual, an active duty Nike Hercules fire control operator assigned to a nuke site, and two Soviet spies in the same room. We need to call the office. But, I don't trust that phone. You stay here while I go to the car and call this in."

"Do not call me a Soviet. I am an ethnic Russian," corrected Nikita.

"Whatever," Norwood said.

He placed the manual inside Jake's pack and handed it to Dikes. "I don't want to be carrying this around. Do you feel okay about being here with Jake and him not being handcuffed?" he asked.

Dikes chuckled, "I can handle Jake. You hurry, and get back here."

Norwood stepped into the hallway, and Dikes locked the door behind him.

"Listen, I am going to pee my pants if you do not let me go to the bathroom. You don't have to take the cuffs off, just put them in front of me so I can take care of my business. Please." Nikita said.

"Not a chance. The handcuffs stay like they are. You can go into the bathroom, pull your dress up and your panties down and sit. The door stays open. That's the deal, take it or leave it," Dikes said.

"Okay, so you like to watch girls do their thing. Pervert," Nikita smirked.

Dikes felt the blood rush to his face. "Go," he said.

Nikita walked to the closed bathroom door and paused. Dikes opened the door, and Nikita stepped inside. She turned and looked at Dikes who was standing in the open doorway. She arched an eyebrow and pulled up her dress. Dikes stepped back and closed the door.

Nikita sat on the toilet. She worked her hands past her hips and down her legs while lifting her feet. She pushed the cuffs down, under and then in front.

She stood and opened the linen cabinet above the toilet. Reaching under the folded towels, she found and removed a Walther PPKS .380 caliber semi-automatic pistol. From behind a second stack, she retrieved a silencer. She screwed the silencer onto the gun.

She flushed the commode and stepped to the side of the bathroom door. The door opened, and Dikes stuck his head inside. "Okay, now get back..." Nikita lifted the pistol and shot the agent in the right eye. He staggered back, and she shot him twice more in the throat.

The pistol was loaded with low-velocity hollow-point rounds. The first round passed through the eye and into the brain. The last two rounds did their work pushing through the soft tissue causing massive hemorrhaging. Thick streams of blood gushed from the great artery in the side of his neck.

Nikita pointed the pistol at Jake and told him, "Don't move or I will shoot you too."

"Get his handcuff key," Demetrio said.

She knelt beside Dikes' body and started rummaging through his pockets in search of the key.

"Robert, let me in," it was Norwood at the door.

Nikita looked to Demetrio for direction. He motioned with his head for her to stand beside the door. He backed to the door so that he could reach the lock with his handcuffed hands. As he turned the lock, Jake shouted, "*She has a gun!*"

It was too late. Norwood pushed open the door as he heard the lock turn. He saw the pistol in Nikita's hand and raised his eyes to look at her. She saw his thoughts as they raced through his mind in the last milliseconds of his life. Surprise, fear, and then resignation flooded through him as he turned his head to look at Dikes lifeless body, lying in his pooled blood.

Nikita fired three quick rounds into the side of the agent's head. She grabbed the lapel of his coat and pulled him forward into the room and let him fall to the floor. She kicked the door closed, pressed the barrel of the pistol to the back of his head and fired the final round through his brain. Special Agent Norwood never heard or felt it.

She laid the pistol down and started searching Dikes' pockets for his handcuff key. Jake sprung forward off the chair, striking Nikita with the full force of his one-hundred and forty-six pounds. The impact bowled her over and knocked the breath out of her.

Demetrio leaped forward and swung his right leg, aiming to hit Jake in the back of his head with his booted foot. As he did, the throw rug beside the bed slipped on the hardwood floor causing him to fall, hitting the back of his head on the unyielding surface.

His boot grazed the side of Jake's head knocking him flat on his face. Jake rolled to his feet, grabbed the lamp beside the bed, and smashed Demetrio in the face with it.

The impact broke Demetrio's nose, and ragged shards of glass filled his eyes. Demetrio blinked, as his eyes filled with blood.

Jake surveyed the mayhem in the room. *'Two dead CID agents and two Russian spies,'* he thought, looking at Nikita.

Glancing at Norwood's body, Jake realized the people the agent had called would be arriving soon. Jake thought about what Demetrio had said. *'Was he an enemy of the State? Would they lock him away and hold him incommunicado for the rest of his life?'* He didn't know the answer to that, but he did know that he could not stay and wait for the arrival of those Norwood had called.

Jake bent over Dikes' body and removed his wallet. He took all of the cash from it and then found the handcuff key and removed it. Next, he took Dikes weapon, removed the bullets and placed them in his pocket. He moved to Norwood's body and did the same.

He looked at Layne, or Nikita, and Demetrio. Both were still dazed. Jake unlocked the handcuff on Layne's left hand and looped it over the links on the cuffs securing Demetrio's hands behind his back. Satisfied he walked to the commode and flushed both handcuff keys.

Jake grabbed his bag, opened the door to check the hallway, and walked out. He locked the door and headed for the stairs.

He paused at the head of the stairs. He did not want to encounter the responding agents in the lobby. He looked around for another exit and saw the window at the end of the hall, leading to the fire escape. He moved to the window, opened it and climbed out onto the metal platform. He realized an open window would point his pursuers to his escape route. He closed the window and hurried down the ladder.

Once on the ground in the alley, Jake stepped behind the dumpster to gather his thoughts. Satisfied that he was alone in the alley, he walked to where it spilled out onto the sidewalk. He looked at the traffic in the street.

He didn't see anyone who looked like government agents, *'but then what would they look like?'* Taking the plunge, Jake stepped from the alley and walked across the street to his car. He opened the trunk and placed his bag inside. He slammed the lid closed, and walked to the driver's side door, opened it and sat down.

'Please,' he thought, *'let this old clunker start.'* He turned the key, the motor over slowly, but then it caught, and blue smoke belched out of the tailpipe. *'That's just great,'* he thought. *'Everyone will be looking at this smoking hulk.'*

Jake checked his mirror, pulled away from the curb, and merged with the traffic. He didn't know where he was going, but he did know that he was leaving one life and entering another.

Jake drove to West, to the campus of the University of Alaska at Fairbanks. He stopped at the Campus Queen, *'Layne, or Nikita, liked this place,'* he remembered.

Inside, he chose a seat by the front window. He kept watching for police cars or any activity to indicate two dead bodies and two living spies had been discovered in the Polaris. He did not see any.

Sipping on his root beer, he thought about the events of the last hour. *'I got away from the Polaris, but now what do I do?'* Jake thought long and hard.

'It is clear that I have no future, other than a dark cell, in the United States. I have nothing to negotiate or bargain with. Except maybe the SOP Manual. They will want to keep it from their enemies.'

Jake felt his face flush hot as a thought came to him, *'Maybe I do have something to bargain with. I have two things going for me. One is the manual. The Soviets would love to get their hands on it. And two, I am an expert on the operations of a Nike Hercules site or at least the operations of the internal fire control van. I hate the idea of being a traitor, but Dikes and Norwood have already classified me as such, and now they are dead. It looks like my best chances lie in the East?'*

His mind made up, Jake left the Campus Queen and drove to the airport. He used his military identification card to purchase a reduced fare ticket to the

Seattle-Tacoma Airport. He was in civilian clothes and was not presenting a military travel voucher, so there was no request for a travel authorization. He had no problem boarding the flight out of Fairbanks.

He forced himself to relax on the flight into Sea-Tac. His reduced fare ticket had him seated in the back of the plane, so he was in the last group to deplane. He walked down the jetway, half expecting to be met by the military police.

As he stepped from the jetway, Jake stood beside the agent's counter. No airline personnel were present. No one paid him any attention. He stood there for a minute looking around the terminal.

"Can I help you find something, soldier?" Jake heard.

He turned to the sound of the voice and saw a skycap standing a few feet from him.

"How did you know I'm a G.I.?" Jake asked.

The skycap laughed and pointed to Jake's shoes. "Those government issued kicks and that skinned head haircut told me."

"Okay," Jake joined in the laugh. "I need to find the pay phones," he said.

"Follow me general," the skycap said and walked away.

Jake followed him to the next intersecting hallway, and the skycap pointed out the bank of pay phones. Jake nodded his thanks and walked to the first phone.

He called information and asked for the number for the Russian embassy. The operator told Jake that there was not a Russian Embassy in Seattle or Tacoma, but there was a Soviet Trade Mission on Beacon Hill. Jake told her that would do and she connected him.

"Soviet Trade Commission," a woman's voice said.

"Good evening. I am an active duty United States soldier and would like to speak with someone about obtaining asylum in the Soviet Union," Jake said.

"Sir, this is the Trade Mission of the U.S.S.R. We do not appreciate prank calls," the woman said.

"I assure you this is no prank call. I am an active duty fire control operator for the Nike Hercules Missile and I have with me the technical specifications for the Nike Hercules, the Standard Operating Procedure, the firing sequence, the alternative sites, the arming and launching codes for all the Nike Hercules sites in the Five-Sixty-Second Air Defense Artillery Battalion of the Alaskan Command," Jake whispered.

That got him some attention. After a short pause, he heard another woman's voice, "Sir, what did you say your name is?"

Jake replied, "I am not ready to give you my name. What I want to know is if you are interested in what I have and what I can provide?"

"Why should I believe that you have the things you say you. Those things would be classified and why would you think the U.S.S.R. would be party to such a seamy affair?" the woman asked.

Jake thought a minute and the woman asked, "Sir, are you still there?"

"Yes, I'm still here. I am going to tell you my name as a show of good faith. My name is Jake Tolbert. If you are not the person I need to talk with, I ask that you get me in touch with that person," Jake said.

She laughed and said, "Mr. Tolbert, or whoever you are, surely you know we are but a trade delegation doing our best to establish peaceful and mutually beneficial commerce between our two great nations."

Fed up with the cat and mouse, Jake said, "Sorry, it looks like I was wrong in thinking you would be interested in what I have. Goodbye."

"*WAIT*, don't hang up. I hear stress in your voice, and I would hate to see you make a foolish mistake," she said. "Wait there by the payphones and let me get back to you."

"How do you know I am calling form a pay phone?" Jake asked.

"Well, surely you can answer that question for yourself," she said.

Jake said, "Whatever. You have exactly thirty minutes. I know the military authorities are already looking for me. It won't take them long to trace my flight out of Fairbanks to here.

I don't intend to stand by and let them lead me to prison. If you are not here in half an hour, I'm gone." Jake hung up the phone and sat down in the

50

chairs next to the bank of pay phones. There was no use in trying to hide.

Twenty-five minutes later a middle-aged man wearing a hat marked 'Yellow Cab' walked up and said, "Jake, I'm your ride."

Jake stood, and followed the man down the main concourse and to the area designated for cabs. The cabbie waved Jake over to his yellow cab. Jake opened the back door and tossed his backpack inside. He slid in and slammed the door.

The driver said, "No, I don't want you sitting back there. I want you up front so I can see you."

Jake smiled, reached over, and grabbed his bag. He exited the cab, closed the back door, and got in the front seat with the cabbie.

The driver started the car and eased out into the flow of traffic. "Where are we going, I don't want to go anywhere except the Soviet Trade Mission," Jake said.

The driver remained silent, keeping his eyes on the traffic. Jake noticed two other cabs pull out and take up positions behind and in front of the one he was in. Another pulled up alongside. The driver of Jake's taxi glanced over at the driver of the cab beside them and nodded. The third cab pulled ahead and led the way for the convoy to the U.S.S.R. Trade Mission.

Jake's cab stopped in front of the Mission. The other three cabs also stopped. One stopped half a block behind the cab Jake was in, one topped half a block ahead, and the third in front of the Mission's gate.

The driver of Jake's cab said, "Get out. Walk straight to the gate. Do not look back at me. Look where you are going. When you reach the gate, a guard will step out of the booth. He will ask how he can help you. You will reply, "I am here to help you." He will open the gate for you; think before stepping through those gates. Once you do, you are on Soviet soil and have surrendered your options."

Jake hesitated a moment and then did as instructed. The gates swung open and Jake stepped from the sovereign soil of his nation onto the sovereign soil of his nation's enemy.

The guard escorted him into the building. He was ushered into a dark room. He heard doors being slammed. Jake, blind as his eyes adjusted to the darkness, was pushed against a wall where strong hands stripped his coat,

51

shirt, and pants from him. A voice whispered in his ear, "Do not resist us. Remain silent and still while we finish our inspection."

Jake nodded his head. The voice returned once again to say, "Sorry, but we must do a full body cavity search. Your mouth first. Open it wide. Good. Now I am going to reach inside with my fingers and move your tongue. Do not bite me. If you do, I promise that you will regret it."

Jake stood still as strange fingers probed his mouth, pulled on his tongue and explored his teeth with the aid of a small flashlight and a slender probe. The examiner pecked on the fillings in his teeth and probed each tooth searching for any communication, tracking or recording device.

"The next part will be unpleasant for both of us and somewhat uncomfortable for you. I don't wish to cause you pain, but I am going to be very thorough; so, as you Americans are prone to say, *'just grin and bear it.'* Now bend over and place your chest on the table in front of you," the voice instructed.

Jake groaned as he heard the sound of a latex glove being snapped into place. Next, he felt the cold jelly applied to his rectum and then the pushing probing fingers violating him, not violently but forcefully just the same.

"He is not carrying anything," the voice said.

"Okay, stand and put your clothes on," a second voice said.

Jake dressed and as he slipped his shoes on, light flooded the room. Jake blinked and glanced around him. Two women stood in front of him.

One of the women spoke, "Follow me. My comrade will be behind you."

Jake recognized the first voice and realized a woman had searched him. He looked into the hard eyes and merely nodded his acceptance of her instruction.

The door opened, and the two women stepped through. Jake followed as they led him upstairs and into a room that looked like a library. His escort pointed to a chair at a table in front of a long shelf of books. Jake sat down, and the doors closed leaving him alone.

Jake sat still. He realized that once the doors closed all the sounds of the building had been blocked out. *'This room is sound proof,'* he thought.

He looked around for any signs of cameras or listening devices. He could see none, but that did not surprise him.

Money, the kind of money a sovereign nation would have available to them would allow the installation of the best equipment in the least obtrusive manner.

The doors swung open, and an elegantly dressed woman entered the room. Jake stood and extended his hand. She shook her head and said, "I do not wish to touch you sir, and you do not need to know my name."

Jake felt his heart sink. He shrugged and sat down. She sat across from him.

"Our specialists have examined your pack and the information the manual contains. They find it interesting; but quite frankly, we already know most of what it provides. What we don't have is your knowledge of how all this works together. We believe you can prove helpful to our cause. Had we not, you would already be in irons awaiting the arrival of your CIA.

"To be completely frank with you, I find one who would betray their nation as you have, to be despicable. I would take great pleasure in pushing you out of our gate and into their arms. However, as I said, that is not the case. You will find a haven with us, as long as you prove useful."

Jake said, "Will I remain here and work with your specialists?"

"No. You will not. We will move you to an area better suited to the purpose. I take it you left in a hurry and do not have a change of clothing, any money and I would guess you have no passport. Am I correct?" she asked.

Jake said, "Yes."

"Fine. You will be shown to a room where you will, and I insist on this, bathe and dress in the clean and respectable clothing provided. Your food will be served to you in the room in which you will be held. Your every need, not wish, but need will be met as we figure out how to get you out of here. Do you have any questions? No, okay," she said turning away from him.

She reached under the table, and Jake heard a buzz. The doors opened, and two men walked in. Neither of them looked at him.

They stopped at the end of the table and stood silently. The woman studied Jake for a few seconds and then faced the men and said, "Take him to the blue room at the top of the stairs. He does not appear to be one who possesses much physical strength, but to be safe, ensure the windows are closed and the bars soundly in place.

Provide him with clothing from the supply. I want two guards outside of his door at all times. You will keep him under constant observation via the closed-circuit cameras. Are my instructions understood? Good. Go now."

Jake stood, and the silent escorts pointed him toward the doors. Jake sighed deeply. His guards looked at each other and laughed.

"You have no idea how your world has changed," one said. My name is Wilhelm, and his name is Janyke. Do as we say, and you will be okay. Attempt to escape, and we will restrain you."

Jake said, "Fair enough, Wilhelm and Janyke. Your names sound German. Are you two from East Germany?"

"We are loyal servants of the Soviet Union, and you are an enemy of our State. That's all you need to know about us, and all we care to know about you. So, don't provoke us," Janyke said.

"I guess that confirms my status," Jake said as he stepped from the room and into his changed world.

Chapter 5

The Quick and The Dead

B.D. Fondren hated having Wednesdays and Thursdays as his days off, but then he was the junior man in his squad.

He graduated from the Army's Criminal Investigation School just three weeks back. He put Hawaii, Florida, and South Carolina on his dream sheet as his choices of assignment. In true army style, some sadist in personnel shipped him to Fort Wainwright, Alaska.

B.D. was unmarried and lived in a furnished apartment off base. Most of his clothing was still in the moving boxes, and he had no food in the pantry or fridge.

B.D. was catching up on some paperwork and watching the clock. The watch-commander had said he could leave early, so he could square away his living quarters.

B.D. saw the watch commander, Chief Warrant Officer, John Johnson, stand and start toward his desk. *'Great,'* B.D. thought, *'he's going to let me go early.'*

As Johnson stepped through the door of the office, his phone rang. He turned and picked the receiver up. B.D. was watching and saw Swenson reach behind him with one hand and slam the door to his office. B.D. sensed this was not a routine call. He watched as Johnson surveyed the office looking from desk to desk. His eyes settled on B.D., and he motioned with his free hand for him to come to the office.

'This does not look good for me leaving early,' thought B.D. He stood and started toward Johnson's office. As he did, Greg Ransome, the senior tenured agent, walked in. Johnson waved him into the office also.

B.D. and Ransome stepped inside Johnson's office and stood before his desk as he finished the telephone conversation. Johnson hung up the phone and asked, "B.D. has your security clearance come through yet?"

B.D. nodded, "Yes it has. I have a top-secret clearance."

"Perfect," Johnson said. "Sit down. This is now a confidential conversation."

B.D. and Ransome looked at each other and sat down. Johnson picked up his phone and dialed.

"This is John T. Johnson for Scott Billings. Tell him this is a priority one call," Johnson spoke into the phone.

Johnson looked at B.D. and Ransome and held his finger to his lips signaling them to sit quietly.

"Hello, John T. What can I do for you," Johnson heard from the receiver.

"Hello, Scott. Maybe you should turn your recorder off before I go into the reason for my call," Johnson said.

"Do you have yours off?" Billings asked.

"Yes, I have turned mine off," Johnson said.

"Alright, mine is off too. I must say you have my interest peaked. What is this all about?" Billings asked.

"This is classified. I just got a call from one of my agents, Archie Norwood. He and his partner, Robert Dikes, have been working a consorting case out of the Five-sixty-second ADA. As you know, their birds are armed with nuclear warheads. The subject of their investigation is an internal fire control operator out of Charlie Battery.

My guys followed the subject into Fairbanks this morning and to make a long story short caught him in a room at the Polaris Club with a man and woman who appear to be Soviet agents. He has top-secret materials relative to the operation of a Nike Hercules site with him. We figure this is now out of our bailiwick and into yours. Thus, this call to you," Johnson explained.

"Thanks, I guess, John T.," Billings laughed into the phone. "My SOP requires I notify Anchorage before involving the bureau. Can you ask your guys to sit on the scene until I can make the call? I'll get right back to you."

"Sure, but Norwood asked for backup. I am going to send two more agents there with the specific instructions to ask nothing, to do nothing, but secure the scene until we hear back from you," Johnson said.

"How are they cleared?" Billings asked.

"They both have top-secret clearances," Johnson replied.

"That will work, but tell them both that this is a no see, no say deal," Billings said and hung up the phone.

Johnson put his phone down, turned to face his agents and said, "You heard the conversation. I want you to go now, get there as soon as you can. They are in room Two-A at the Polaris.

Ransome, you are the senior agent. Take charge as soon as you step into the room. I don't want you to ask any questions. All I want you to do is secure the scene until we can hand this off to the FBI. Got it?"

"Got it, boss," Ransome said and headed for the door.

"I just turned my car in, do you have one?" Ransome asked B.D.

B.D. nodded, "Yep, sitting out front."

"Good, do you know where the Polaris is?" Ransome asked.

"Yes, I do. My first case was a one where a G.I. assaulted one of the whores over there," B.D. replied.

"Let's go then and step on it. We need to get there, ASAP," Ransome said.

B.D. and Ransome trotted to the car and headed out. As they approached the front gate of Fort Wainwright, Ransome reached over and flicked the red lights in the grill on and off.

The M.P. working outbound traffic stepped in front of those waiting to exit the Fort and held up his hand stopping the flow of cars. He pointed to the outside lane and waved the CID Agents through.

As they approached the Polaris they could see that the street was lined, every parking slot taken. "Double park it and put the placard on the dash," Ransome said.

B.D. stopped the car and Ransome jumped out running for the front door. B.D. placed the placard reading, "CID Fort Wainwright" in the windshield and followed. Ransome was knocking on the door when B.D. reached the second floor.

"Something's wrong. Go back downstairs and get the key from the front desk. Don't take any slack, get that key and get back up here with it," Ransome said.

B.D. ran down the stairs and over to the desk. Reaching inside his coat pocket, he withdrew his credentials and waved them in front of the clerk. "Give me the key to Two-A now," he said.

The startled clerk reached behind the desk and took the key from the pegboard on the wall. Handing it to B.D., she asked, "Is everything okay?"

"Everything is fine," B.D. said. He took the stairs, two at a time, and ran to the door. He inserted the key and felt Ransome's hand on his arm. Looking up he saw Ransome holding his pistol and motioning him to stand at the side of the door.

B.D. stepped aside, out of the line of fire, and drew his pistol. Ransome reached over and turned the key in the lock. B.D. pushed the door open.

The smell of gunpowder, and blood washed over the agents. B.D. stopped, blocking the entrance into the room.

Ransome realized the young agent had frozen and reached up to push him through the door. Ransome stepped into the room behind B.D. and said, "Snap out of it kid. I need you with me here."

B.D. felt his stomach heave and knew he was not going to be able to hold it. He took one step toward the open door of the bathroom and spewed the contents of his stomach across the bed.

He heard a gasp and saw movement just below the top of the bed and realized someone was hiding on the far side. Ransome saw it too and said, "Live or die, it's your choice. Show me your hands."

B.D. wiped his mouth and chin with the back of his left sleeve while raising his pistol with his right.

"Show me those hands," Ransome demanded again.

"We can't, we're handcuffed together one in front and one in the back," came a woman's voice.

"Stand then, and face the wall," Ransome said.

Nikita and Demetrio staggered to their feet. Nikita's face was covered with the vomit B.D. had spewed across the bed.

58

B.D. watched as it dripped from her forehead and nose down across her lips and chin. Nikita tried to spit it away but as she opened her lips the vomit ran inside her mouth, and she retched. B.D. felt his stomach turn and gagged.

"Damn it boy, get a grip," Ransome demanded.

B.D. took a deep breath, nodded and said, "Got it, I'm okay."

"Check Norwood and Dikes," Ransome ordered.

B.D. kneeled over Dikes and checked for a pulse. He found none. He moved to Norwood and repeated the procedure. Rising to his feet, he looked at Ransome and said, "They're both dead."

Ransome pulled the hammer back on his pistol and raised it to point directly at Demetrio's face. "You get one chance to tell me what happened here. Let's start with why you killed them?"

Nikita pulled herself up as straight as she could and looking Ransome full in the eye she said, "He didn't kill them. It was me. I shot them both."

Ransome shook his head slowly, looking at Demetrio, "I don't believe you. I don't think a little woman like you could take them both. I think it was him."

Nikita laughed, "You stupid Americans. You are such chauvinists. This issue was not determined by size. It was a matter of how do you say, the quick and the dead. I was the quicker, and they are the dead. It is as simple as that."

"Put that gun down," spoke a voice from the doorway.

B.D. and Ransome both wheeled toward the sound to see two men in suits striding into the room closing the door behind them.

"You fools why did you leave the door open? Has anyone seen this mess?" the first man asked.

"Who are you?" Ransome asked.

"I'm Special Agent Zack Mayfield, and this is my partner, Special Agent David Box. We're from the Fairbanks office of the F.B.I. and this is now our scene," the taller of the two men standing before them said.

"Show me your credentials," Ransome demanded.

Both men extended a badge and identification card showing them to be Special Agents of the Federal Bureau of Investigation.

Ransome and B.D. holstered their weapons and Ransome said, "By God it's yours. All we want is our agent's bodies."

"No, I'm sorry. I know how you feel, but nothing is to be moved. That includes your agents' bodies. They stay where they fell, for now. You are now witnesses in a National Security Case and will be placed in protective custody," Mayfield said.

"You are placing us in protective custody? No way. I want to call my office," Ransome said.

"No. Now calm down and think with me. Put yourself in my shoes. I must place you in protective custody so that I contain all of this within the four walls of this room.

Work with me, I know and respect your position but you are still in service, and I need your cooperation. Trust me, and I will take care of you and see to it your dead agents receive the respect they deserve," Mayfield said.

Ransome thought a minute and said, "He's right B.D. Let's handle this right."

"Thanks, guys. Now let's work this out," Mayfield said.

Turning to Box, Mayfield said, "Go to the car and get on the radio. Turn the scrambler on. Tell the boss what we have and ask for a team to clean this scene. Tell him that we need two body bags, and transport.

Tell him we will need four men to work these bodies down the fire escape. Tell him we have two foreign agents in custody. Tell him I will let him know where I am taking them once I have the facts of this incident."

Box hastened from the room, and Mayfield locked the door behind him. Turning to Nikita and Demetrio, he said, "Let me be frank with you. As of this minute, you do not exist, you are going to disappear within our system.

The world will never know about any of this, so don't expect us to treat you with deference to world opinion or expectations. You are foreign agents who have murdered active duty personnel of the United States Army. We can execute you and be within the law.

60

But then, as I said, you do not exist so we have a lot of options. We can take our time and slowly strip from you every piece of information you have. We can employ all the techniques, all the enhanced interrogation methods we need to and no one will know. Are you following me so far?"

Nikita nodded and said, "Yes, we understand what you have said, please continue."

"You will never again be free, that you already know. You should not worry about what your countrymen will think of you because you no longer have a country. You have a choice. You can cooperate and live out your captivity in relative ease. Or you can resist us and live the rest of your life in pain. Which shall it be?" he asked.

Nikita looked at Demetrio. She could see that he was struggling to remain conscious. She knew he was not able to make an informed decision, so she turned to Mayfield and asked, "Will you guarantee that we will not be executed or turned over to our countrymen after you finish with us?"

Mayfield nodded, "Yes, I will guarantee that. You will be a permanent guest of the United States government and will die of old age locked away within a mountain in the Western United States."

"How dreary," Nikita said. "But still, it is better than a closed coffin in the cold ground or being turned over to the KGB. We have a deal. Now get us out of here. As you can see Demetrio needs a physician."

Box knocked on the door, and Mayfield let him in. "The boss said it is your show. The resources you asked for are on the way." Box licked his lips and looked at Ransome and B.D.

"Anything else?" Mayfield asked.

"Yes. The boss said to tell you that he is on the line with the Department of the Army arranging to have these dead agents' records altered to show that they are on special assignment. He said that it is to remain so until the Bureau says otherwise," Box replied.

Mayfield turned to Ransome, "I take it you're senior here," he said.

"That's right," Ransome said.

"You understand what this means? There will be no acknowledgment of their death. We want to keep this from the Soviets as long as possible. As tragic as this is, we must exploit it for all it's worth.

I am sorry. The time will come when we can honor your agents and their sacrifice for the nation, but not now," Mayfield said.

Ransome dropped his head, "We understand. Let's get them up off that floor and out of here as soon as possible."

There was a knock at the door as Ransome spoke. Mayfield asked, "Who is it?"

"It is the clean Team," was the response from the other side of the door.

"Let them in," Mayfield said to Box.

Box opened the door, and the team stepped inside. Mayfield pointed to the bodies of Norwood and Dikes, "These are ours. Treat them with dignity. Make them disappear for now, but keep them where we can do the right thing when it's time. The rest of you put this room right. I want no signs that this ever happened. Go to it and make it quick?"

Then he said, "Box, get the handcuffs on these two straightened out. I want their hands in front of them so they can have better balance when we take them down the fire escape. You will hold them in the alley behind that big green dumpster until I can get the car and pull it around. Let's go."

Chapter 6

Orders

He was flying, soaring high above the desert floor. He spread his arms and legs allowing the thermal updrafts full access to his naked body. The hot air soothed his frozen bones. He never wanted to see Alaska again.

J.B. woke, tangled in his sweat-soaked sheets. Hot air blasting from the overhead vent filled his small room, pushing the temperature beyond the point of tolerance.

He kicked the sheets off his wet body, and stood. His skivvies and undershirt stuck to his skin. The luminous dial on his GI watch showed it to be three o'clock. *'Well I will be go to hell,'* he thought, *'I've been asleep just two hours and guard mount is in two more. This is going to be a long day.'*

Walking over to the window he pulled back the curtains and opened the blinds. The dazzling glare of lights bouncing off the snow filled the room. He glanced at the thermometer stuck to the corner of the window and saw that it read fifty-five degrees below zero.

Standing there staring through the ice fog at the frozen grounds of Fort Wainwright, J.B. allowed his thoughts to roll back over the events that brought him to this stop in his destiny.

It all started on a day in late November of 1967. He stepped from his car to see an envelope sticking up out of the mailbox on his porch. His first thought was, *'that's odd, almost like the carrier wanted to be sure I saw that letter.'*

Warily he pulled the envelope out of the box. There in the upper left corner he saw stamped, *United States Selective Service, Local Board 22, McKinney, Texas.*

J.B. opened the envelope and stood there on the porch to read the Board's instructions for him to report for a physical examination at the Armed Forces Examination and Entrance Station in Dallas. The letter was dated November 20, 1967.
The Vietnam War was raging, and chewing up men at a phenomenal rate.

J.B. sighed, remembering the physical. He, and a room full of other young men, were told to strip to their shorts. A grizzled old sergeant ordered them

63

into a single line. An army physician passed in front of the men spending maybe two minutes looking into their eyes, their ears, or thumping here and there on them and then moving on to the next man.

Having traversed the line, the physician asked "Is there any man here who wants to claim a physical disability that will disqualify him for military service?"

Several men did so. The physician turned and moved away a few paces. Taking his cue, the old master sergeant stepped up and walked along in front of those claiming a disability.

As he stood in front of the first man, he smiled and then leaned forward in a fatherly manner. J.B. chuckled as he remembered all thoughts of affection or politeness vanished as the sergeant unleashed a vile, profane description of one who would seek to avoid service under the flag of the greatest nation in the history of the world.

By the time his tirade was over, half of the men had stepped back into line. The others stood their ground but dared not look at the sergeant as he growled to the physician, "Sir, we have some slackers here for your attention. I have scrutinized each of these men and based on my thirty years of experience, which includes combat in World War II and Korea, I don't believe any of them have a disability. But, that is your decision sir."

The sergeant moved back respectfully, and the physician nodded as he again strolled along the line of those who dared hold out for a closer physical exemption.

Stopping in front of one, he whispered, "Open your mouth and stick your tongue out."

The man did as instructed, and the physician said, "Sergeant, please note that this man has excellent hearing, and is able to understand and follow bifurcated instructions.

Also make a note that I can see that he practices good dental hygiene and that he has excellent control of his tongue. I find him qualified for service. Step back with the rest of the men, son."

The next man he stopped in front of smiled at the physician and said, "Doctor..."

The sergeant came running at the man screaming, "Shut your mouth. You will speak when told to speak. And when you do speak to the Captain, you will address him as, sir."

The physician said, "Now Son, I want you to drop your shorts, grasp your right testicle with your right hand, turn your head to the left and cough for me."

The man followed the instructions as given, and the physician asked, "When you coughed did you feel any pain or discomfort in your testicular sack?"

The examinee cast his eyes over to the sergeant who nodded and said, "Answer the Captain, maggot."

"No sir, I didn't feel any discomfort, sir," he was finally able to croak.

The Captain smiled and said, "Excellent. You pass. Step back with the other men."

And with that, the man had passed his physical examination.

And so, it had gone. After the doctor had finished his examination and all of them were once again in a single line, he said to the sergeant, "Now Sergeant, let's take a closer look to be sure they are all sound in their backsides."

The sergeant stepped forward and said, "Turn and face the wall behind you. Drop your shorts and let them hit the floor. Step out of them, leave them laying where they fall, and wait for further instructions."

Every mother's son turned and dropped their shorts. Then came the next command, "Bend over, grab your ankles and stick your head between your knees. I want to see that spot where the sun does not shine.

The Captain here must take a look for any abnormalities. He will not touch you, but he will be walking along behind you.

Every once in a while, we have some joker who thinks it would be funny to spray the good Captain with some personal gas. If you do, I promise that you will regret it every day for the rest of your military life."

The Captain plodded along behind the men. Each of them had waited anxiously with their bottoms bared and red faces turned up as he trooped the line using a small flashlight to splash a beam of light across their rectums.

His inspection finished the Captain said, "Sergeant, every man here is an excellent example of the perfect rectum and therefore uniquely qualified for military service."

Three weeks later J.B. opened another letter from the Selective Service. This one read: *From The President of The United States of America. To: Jacob Babb Gideon, 1709 M Place Plano, Texas. Greetings, You have been selected by your friends and neighbors to serve in the Armed Forces of the United States. You are now instructed and required to report for induction at the Federal Building in McKinney, Texas on the second of January 1968 at 5:00 a.m. sharp. Herein fail not, under the penalty of law.*

J.B. knew that as an active duty police officer for the City of Dallas, he was considered to be engaged in a critical public safety occupation and would be granted an exemption from service by merely asking for it. He considered it, but could not find in himself to do so. Not with so many giving so much in this war. He had to go. And that was how this odyssey had begun.

Next came eight weeks of hell at Fort Polk, Louisiana. The days started at four-thirty a.m., and ended when the Drill Sergeants ran out of sadist ideas. Each day repeated the one before; they ran five miles before breakfast, had forced marches in full gear, crawled sand pits under live fire, stood in rooms filled with gases designed to cause you to retch with burning eyes and itching skin, and endured cursing, screaming and the occasional boot in the bottom when the Drill Sergeant wasn't satisfied with your effort.

J.B. had a double dose of the Drill Sergeants' ire once they found out that he had been a Dallas Police Officer before being drafted. His Drill Sergeant was forever yelling, "Where is my cop?" J.B. remembered the first day. The drill sergeant stood in front of him and asked, "What is your prefix?"

J.B. responded, "U.S., drill sergeant."

"Draftee, you are a draftee. You don't want to serve your country, is that right scum bag?" the drill sergeant screamed.

"No, drill sergeant. I could have had an exemption, but I did not choose to exercise that option, drill sergeant," J.B. replied.

"Why could you have had an exemption, maggot?" the drill sergeant asked.

"Because I was an active duty police officer, drill sergeant," J.B. answered.

J.B. saw the drill sergeant's eyes narrow and knew he had made a big mistake.

The drill sergeant stepped in and leaned forward until the brim of his hat was resting on the bridge of J.B.'s nose. He then screamed, "A cop. I have a cop in my platoon. I hate cops, do you hear me, maggot? I promise you that I will make every day of your life here at Fort Polk a living hell. Do you hear me, maggot?"

"Yes, drill sergeant, I hear you," J.B. responded.

The hell started at three a.m. the next morning when J.B. reported for kitchen police duties. At ten-thirty that night, he limped into the barracks, pulled his grimy fatigues off and crawled into his bunk. His second day in hell started six and one-half hours later when the drill sergeant turned his bed over dumping him onto the floor. Day after day the drill sergeant kept his word.

J.B. entered basic training weighing two hundred and twenty-two pounds. He left weighing 164 and so hoarse from screaming, "Yes, Drill Sergeant," that he could barely speak.

What kept him going was a day in the middle of training when he was pulled aside to meet with two men in civilian clothing.

His Drill Sergeant wanted to be present, but the men in civilian clothing would have none of it.

They each produced badges and instructed the Drill Sergeant to leave the area. The Drill Sergeant drifted away, but J.B. could tell that he was going to catch the brunt of his frustration once the interview was over.

The men introduced themselves as special agents from the Criminal Investigations detachment of the Military Police at Fort Polk, and explained that he had been selected for the Military Police Corps. In short, they were to verify his identity, and that he had been an active duty police officer before being drafted. They also wanted to confirm that he was not married, and had no siblings.

Then came questions about him sharing his name with an uncle who was highly decorated for actions behind German lines during World War II. That uncle had hit his lieutenant and served some time in Leavenworth. Satisfied that J.B. was not apt to strike an officer, they cleared him for the Corps.

Two weeks later, J.B. was ordered to report to his training company commander. Different men in civilian clothing were waiting in the Captain's office. The Captain told J.B. that the men were with the government and that he was to answer their questions. The Captain then left him alone with the men.

Once again J.B. found himself being interviewed and interrogated at the same time. These two told him they were with the F.B.I. and were there to complete his background investigation. They needed to ask a couple more questions for their final report.

What followed was two hours of questioning concerning his growing up in Plano, his time at the University of Texas at El Paso and his excursions across the border into Juarez. Once again, they were especially interested in his war hero uncle.

They told J.B. that he was selected for a specialized training program at Fort Lewis Washington, once he completed basic training. The agents told him to expect to be separated from his company immediately after graduation.

He would be assigned to a separate barracks and held in isolation until his escort arrived to take him to his next assignment. He was to tell no one of his assignment, and if pressed he was to refer the questioner to their office.

The escort came for him in the middle of a rainy night. J.B. was sleeping in an empty barracks, and he remembered them coming in so silently that he did bit hear them approach. A rough hand on his shoulder and a flashlight shining in his face woke him. They asked his name, checked his dog tags and told him to get up, dress and come with them.

J.B. dressed quickly and turned to pack his duffle bag. "Leave it," the big one said.

"All of it?" J.B. asked.

"Everything," was the reply. "Don't worry about it. Just come with us, and there is no need for more conversation," they were polite but firm.

That's how he left Fort Polk. The next morning found him standing in the rain with a group of other recruits in the middle of a national forest outside Fort Lewis Washington.

A jeep delivered four sergeants in fatigues, and polished helmet liners with MP emblazoned across the front. One sergeant ordered the recruits to fall in, dress right and then to stand at ease. He introduced himself and the other sergeants as their cadre for the segment of their training.

It soon became apparent that all of the recruits were draftees. They were told that the war in Vietnam was demanding more and more infantrymen and that those demands were being met principally from the draftees entering active duty each month.

The result was that the military police school was not getting enough men to fill the army's need for law enforcement. In order to fill the need, the army decided to draft experienced civilian police officers who would be able to step into the police duties straight out of their basic military training.

The training command realized that keeping police officers from the same state together would provide a cohesive unit, which would acclimate to the military function quicker. So here they were.

J.B. listened, but knew there was more to this than they were being told. If the army needed them for law enforcement then why were they here in the middle of a forest and what was the *"military function"* the sergeant referred to?

The training began immediately and the brutality of the next eight weeks made those at Polk pale in comparison.

J.B. laughed, remembering the Drill Sergeants at Polk pushing them to the point of exhaustion, screaming and kicking recruits who fell out. There had been one-on-one combat training with pugil sticks, in the sawdust pits with controlled throws and pulled punches.

But here, there was no sawdust, there were no pulled punches or controlled throws, and you never knew when an attack was coming. You had better keep your head on a swivel and be ready at every instant, or someone was going to do you some serious bodily harm.

He became skilled in special weapons and tactics, dismounted and unarmed combat and learned what it meant to run. His one hundred and sixty-four pounds soon melted away to one hundred and forty-five pounds of muscle and bone. He learned how to survive in the forests and they were told that the next phase would be crucial to their assignment.

It was an intense course in land navigation, escape and evasion tactics and

69

some fundamental enhanced interrogation techniques to be used for the expeditious gleaning of information deemed critical to the survival of units actively engaged in combat operations.

J.B. remembered wincing when hearing that term, "combat operations." *'Why in the hell did they need all of this training if they were going to be military police officers?'*

Six weeks later he and his fellow trainees learned how to exit a Huey as it hovered over a landing zone. They practiced moving quickly from the landing zone to the target, accomplishing the mission and running to the extraction point.

The interrogation techniques were brutal and required one to become disconnected with the conventions of civilization. To use them required one to view the subject as nothing more than the source of desired information.

Nothing was off limits when it came to *'exploiting the source.'* Nothing.

Then before dawn one morning they boarded a chopper and were flown onto the main post at Fort Lewis where they received a short orientation to the Military Police service, as contrasted to their civilian police officer training.

Each man was assigned to a brief stint with the Armed Forces Police detachment working the Seattle Tacoma airport. Next, they worked with a unit chasing AWOL's (soldiers absent from their assignment without proper leave) and deserters across the Pacific North West.

Then, without prior notice, they were loaded onto an Air Force C-130 and transported to Eielson Air Force Base outside Fairbanks, Alaska. There they were loaded on trucks and taken to Fort Wainwright.

J.B. woke that first morning at Wainwright to a bone-chilling minus thirty degrees. After breakfast, the newly arrived troops were issued their arctic gear and loaded onto helicopters for a trip into the mountain wilderness north of Fairbanks.

Here they received thirteen weeks of training in Arctic Warfare, which included a concentration on surreptitious insertion into hostile territory and instruction on the capture and removal of designated *'targets'* back to friendly soil.

Following their training, they were returned to Fort Wainwright, and

70

assigned routine Military Police duties with the Four-Seventy-Second Military Police Company. The routine did not lasted long, before the insertions and removals began.

———————————————————

J.B. heard steps approaching and then a knock at his door. "Who's pecking on my door in the middle of the night," he called.

"It's me, Elias," was the answer.

"What do you want?" J.B. asked.

"You have orders, sergeant," Elias said.

"Orders is it? Well, don't keep me waiting. Get in here with them," J.B. barked.

The door opened, and Elias walked in. "Sorry, Sarge," he said as he handed J.B. a sheaf of papers.

J.B. looked at the top page.

Gideon, Jacob Babb Sgt. E-5, US 54443294, is detached from the 472 Military Police Company Ft. Wainwright Alaska, USARAL and assigned (TDY) to the 562 Military Police Group (Provisional) USARAL effective 3 January 1969.

He flipped to the back page and saw what he was looking for. *"By order of Gillis B. Ost, Colonel, USARAL, Ft. Wainwright Commanding."*

J.B. looked up at Elias and asked, "Any calls yet?"

Elias nodded, "Lieutenant Groves called about half an hour ago. He will be here for you at five a.m. He said for you to leave all your identification in your duffel, be dressed in your TA-Fifty and standing at the door ready to move north."

J.B. recognized the name Groves. At least he wouldn't have to break a lieutenant in.

"Okay, Elias," J.B. said. "Same drill as last time. I will lock the room as I leave, drop a key on the front desk and expect everything to be as I left it, when I get back. My instructions and letters to the family will be on the desk in a sealed envelope in the event I don't make it. Got it?"

Elias nodded again. His mouth worked as if he wanted to speak, but nothing came out. J.B. slapped him on the shoulder and winked. Elias shrugged and walked away.

J.B. packed his room, shaved, showered, and sat down to write his farewells. At four-thirty, he put his notes into an envelope, sealed it, and placed it in the middle of the desk where it could be easily seen.

He dressed in his fatigue pants and OG shirt, pulled on shell pants, lined with sheep wool, and then the white bunny boots.

He picked up his parka, his mittens, a mask, and headed for the front door. As he stepped into the foyer, he could see the deuce and a half idling out front.

He shrugged into the parka, pulled a wool skullcap down tight, and stepped into the frost.

Chapter 7

Crossing Over

The tailgate dropped, and the canvas was pulled back as J.B. approached the truck. A mitten-covered hand was extended through the gap. J.B. grasped it and pulled himself up and inside the truck. He secured the tailgate, closed the flaps and turned to face the lone occupant.

First Lieutenant Sam Groves sat on a canvas bench. He picked up his radio and pressed the transmitter bar, breaking squelch, then laid it down without speaking. The truck began to move forward.

J.B. sat down across from Groves. Neither man spoke for a minute. Then Groves said, "You're going across again."

J.B. leaned back, "I figured as much. I noticed that you didn't say us. Does that mean you are not going?"

Groves shook his head, "Not this time."

"You know I only have two months left on this tour, right boss?" J.B. asked.

"I know, and I wish it were possible to let you slide on this but I can't," the Lieutenant said with a tight smile.

"Okay. When and where?" J.B. asked.

"That is to be determined, but it will be soon. Your target is moving. If our intelligence is right, you should be able to intercept him on Big Diomede. We will have to insert you at no more than four clicks."

"Four clicks! Whoa, now boss. That's not an insertion that is an invasion. Why the big change? We've never done anything but coastal stuff before, at the water's edge. Now you're sending us inland? Why," J.B. asked.

The Lieutenant did not respond, so J.B. continued, "Nothing can move on that island without the NKVD knowing. They will be all over us. Damn it, we will be in a kill zone no matter where we sit down. This just can't be done, boss."

"Orders say we will, that means we can," the Lieutenant said.

J.B. was fuming. But discipline took over, and he calmed himself and said, "I know that, Sir. But if you will allow me, this doesn't smell right.

The last four times, we were inserted and escorted a team of spooks out. Or provided security for a team taking a quick look at something or setting up a listening post. Those actions were all on the coast, not inland.

You are talking about targets inland at four clicks. Four clicks puts us near their counterintelligence center on Big Diomede. It also suggests that we are going to have to bring this target out.

What's up here boss, obviously this is no escort or security gig. Who is this target and what are our orders?"

"Your target is a deserter from the Five-sixty-second who killed or is connected somehow to the death of two Army CID agents, and the theft of classified information. He has defected to the Soviet bloc.

Command fears he will assist them in using the stolen information to defeat our air defenses protecting Eielson.

We believe the Soviets are moving him to their counterintelligence center on Big Diomede to use him in breaking our arming, and firing codes for the Nike Hercules deployed here, also along the west coast and across the lower forty-eight. Our orders are to intercept him, bring him and the stolen information out, or kill him. No witnesses will be left alive. It is as simple as that sergeant," Groves' face was hard.

J.B. sat still, thinking about how dangerous this mission was going to be and how little time he had left on this tour of duty.

"Help me understand something. Why us? Why not Special Forces or the Special Ops bunch out of Fort Lewis," J.B. asked

"Time is one reason. It would take too long to assemble a force from Lewis, and get them on station. Secondly, this guy is out of the Five-sixty-second and we are the military police group responsible for the Five-sixty-second. He is a deserter, and he killed two of our own. That makes this our job. He is our responsibility. Agreed, Sergeant?" the Lieutenant asked.

J.B. shrugged and nodded his head, "Yes Sir," he answered.

"Good. Now, let's talk about where you will sit down. One option is Big Diomede, but there is also the option of you jumping off from our place on Little Diomede and being inserted south of Alyatki.

74

You would intercept him as they move him to the ferry for the trip to the island," Groves said.

"Big Diomede would put us in at four klicks. Alyatki is more like fifty-eight klicks. That is even more of an invasion," Gideon retorted, and then paused for the Lieutenant to respond.

When he didn't J.B. continued, "The thing about Alyatki is it gives us more cover and a hell of lot more room to run and hide.

But listen LT. , you have been across before. You know how thick the maritime patrol boats are around the big island, especially on the south side. We'd be taking fire on the way in. That would bring the MVD running. It would be a blood bath."

"I have thought about that," Groves said. "What if I call the boss and suggest that we stick with the plan to stage at our place on Little Diomede.

When we get the green light, we have two slicks lift off at the same time. One will fly high and bright, with lots of radio noise, toward Katzebue.

The watchers and their border police will think it is nothing but a routine flight along our side of the line; then, about fifteen minutes out, we have them stray over the line a couple of klicks. That will get everybody's attention and cause the watchers to focus on that chopper.

This provides a screen for you in the second slick. It will swing southwest to clear land. It will then loop around to the North side of the big island. The pilot will take you inland, set you down, lift off to the northwest, and head for Nome.

If we keep him skimming the waves at top speed, it is a good bet we can get back across the strait without them ever seeing him.
What do you think?"

J.B. sat mulling the plan over, and then said, "Okay, that kind of diversion might work. They will never expect an insertion that far north.

But then after we hit them, we will have a long run to the extraction point, or the bird will have to pick us up at the ambush site. The flight out will take us right over their SAM's.

A better idea is for us to hit them outside the intelligence center, run to an

75

extraction point on the coast and fly out to link up with our gunboats at the midpoint. They could provide fire support if needed, and once we cross into our waters, our jets could splash any pursuers."

Groves said, "Agreed, we will go in low and fast. The LZ should be cold giving you a chance to form up and be on station before our target arrives. You have to take him north of the center and in no circumstances can you let him get behind those walls.

We want to bring him back, but if that becomes impossible, you are to kill him. You know that you will have to kill the escort, too.

Take some time to harvest any hard intelligence you find on the bodies, and then run south and west to the extraction point."

"And if the LZ is not cold?" J.B. asked.

"Once you leave that chopper, you are on your own. It is up to you to make sure before you exit the aircraft," Groves said.

"Yeah sure, and of course we go clean," J.B. said.

"Totally," Groves responded.

"Then that's the plan," Groves said, and continued without giving J.B. a chance to respond, "Sergeant, I know that this is more than a little outside of what we have done in the past, especially in the fact that you are going to have to use lethal force to accomplish this mission. But remember that this is what we trained your unit for in the forest there outside of Fort Lewis.

Our Command Staff has made the decision that we are going to do this. And, they want us to send a message in doing it.

That message is this, you may hit us, you may hurt us, you may compromise our security, but there will be a payback. We will come for you, and you will not escape us. Borders will not stop us, and governments will not shield you."

J.B. sat a minute and then said, "Sounds more like an Israeli response than one from us."

"Well, maybe it's time we start thinking and acting more like Israel. Is it simple and is it brutal?

76

You damned right it is! But that's what it has come to if we are to survive as a nation," Groves said.

"Okay, sir, so you have opened this up. Do I now have permission to speak?"

"Sure, go ahead," Groves said.

"This is an espionage case, and that is what the NSA, the FBI, and the CIA are for. We are field MP's, not intelligence agents and for damned sure, not assassins," J.B. responded.

Groves sat back and sighed. He looked at J.B. for a few seconds and then said, "I am going to indulge you and discuss these details with you, but we have orders, and we are going to follow them. Aren't we sergeant?"

J.B. nodded.

Groves thought a minute and then said, "First, you have to understand that Fairbanks is full of spies. They watch everything we do, including troop movements, especially our special ops teams. They would detect our operation, and the alert would go out. That decreases the odds of success.

Second, as I said earlier, this theft of top-secret information occurred on our watch. This deserter is out of the Battalion we are assigned to police and thus our responsibility. He is shredding our national security, and we need him stopped.

The spies know that we on occasion move from the Four-Seventy-Second to augment the Five-Sixty-Second on TDY and so this move will not be all that interesting to them. They will not be watching us because to them we are just another group of MP's.

We will make the insertion, accomplish the mission and be back before they know it.

Now about the target, his name is Jake Tolbert. I hate to tell you this, but he is a Texan.

He was assigned as a scope dope in the internal fire control center at Charlie Battery of the Air Defense Artillery Battalion protecting the SAC base at Eielson," Groves said, and J.B. could tell he was choosing his words carefully.

The Lieutenant continued, "Three weeks ago, Charlie Battery was hot, and he was on the scope. Somehow, he managed to walk out with the specs on their missiles, the SOP for the Integrated Fire Control System, the arming codes and firing order for all five batteries of the Five-sixty-second. Then he disappeared.

We have learned that he flew to Seattle where he boarded a flight for Seoul. We lost him once he left the airport. Two days later he turned up in the North where he boarded a Russian Military flight..."

"And let me finish it for you," J.B. interrupted, "That is why the brass thinks he is headed for their electronic warfare center across the Bering Strait from us.

From that vantage point, he will be able to assist them in finding a way to disarm our birds while they are still in the pits or to jam them in flight before they have radar acquisition of a target.

But they can't launch or detonate them because we will have already changed all of those codes. They must know that."

"That's right," Groves said.

"So then doesn't this all become academic, an exercise in futility. I mean sir, even if they can get past the problem with the codes they still would need the validation key, and those are changed with each duty officer," J.B. said.

" Yes, that's right. As I said before he gave them the codes but he could not give them the validation key because the duty officer changes it every cycle.

When a firing order is given, the officer in the pit where the birds are stored will not allow the bird to be armed or released without that key. The keys follow a sequence of numbers, letters, and symbols. Individual officers tend to favor and repeat a given sequence to complete the key.

The key is transmitted via what is supposed to be a secure line from the internal fire control van to the duty officer in the pits. He enters the key into the fire control computer, and the bird is free to fly," Groves explained.

"And this traitor knows the individual officers' tendencies, which will give their computer geeks a start on figuring out the validation key or keys, is that what you are saying?" J.B. asked.

"That's it. It will take them some time, but our intelligence guys believe that he knows these operations so well that he will be able to build the whole process for them.

Once they have a list of the possibilities all they have to do is jam our birds until they hit the right sequence and validation key. They then can arm or disarm the bird in the pit or the air, just as you have described," the Lieutenant said.

"The weak link appears to be the duty officers who tend to repeat the same sequence in the validation keys. So why not just replace the duty officers," J.B. asked.

Groves responded, "We are working on that, but these guys don't grow on trees. Remember these are Nike Hercules missiles. And they are armed with nuclear warheads.

The only others, with nukes, in the U.S. are in Florida. Those boys are holding the line on Castro, and his Russian buddies camped out ninety miles away. Those duty officers are qualified, but cannot be moved.

The next closest officers, qualified on these birds, are in Germany. But we can't strip those batteries of their fire control officers. It is going to take some time to get qualified officers posted here. In the meantime, we have to keep these guys on station. And yes, we are on them to change their tendencies. But..."

J.B. interrupted, "Okay, so once again, let's just send in an assassin, hit this guy, and he tells nobody anything."

"No, because we want to know, if possible, how much he has given them. We can then adjust for that and move on," Groves said.

"Okay boss, if you say so, but I have to tell you this makes no sense to me. We can change all these operations, codes and stuff. Sure, it causes a little extra work on the scope dopes and pit rats but which is better, their effort in a secure area or our blood in the snow.

Is that the message we want the world to see. And by the way, if we want the whole world to know that we hit this guy then why do we go in stripped of identifying information?" J.B. asked.

Grooves leaned back, looked at the sergeant, and said, "J.B., do you believe that there is anyone in the communist world who will not know we crossed over and dealt justice?"

Groves continued without waiting for J.B. to answer, "And it has become apparent that you are missing an important point here.

This is about sending a message, yes, but it is also about the security of the west coast. You don't know these Nikes and what role they play in our first line of defense, do you? Don't answer; just listen and learn something here.

Groves took a deep breath and then said, "The Nike Hercules MIM-Fourteen is a solid fuel, ground-controlled guided missile deployed principally as a surface to air SAM-Twenty-five or in the army's vernacular, Air Defense Artillery.

They have a range of seventy-seven miles, fly at speeds in excess of Mach three-point-six-five and are capable of carrying a twenty-kilotonne nuclear or five hundred and two kilotonne high explosive conventional warhead. We have five batteries of them deployed around Eielson to protect our bombers stationed there. They can take down airborne missiles or inbound planes.

If the Russians decide to send their Bear Bombers across the Bering Strait, we launch the Nike Hercules and vaporize their planes with an airburst right in the middle of the formation. Or if they send ground troops we simple reconfigure the bird, and it becomes a cannon.

We fire it into their midst with a six-hundred-pound High Explosive Fragmentation load, and it will clear a path half a mile wide. We have closed their invasion route with these Nike Hercules, and they know it.

But we do have a problem, and they know that also. The integrated fire control area of the Nike Hercules System contains the radars and computers driving the operation of the missile site.

Locking onto the target has to be done manually by varying the range, elevation, and azimuth of the target tracking radar.

After the target is acquired, the system can monitor the missile and target automatically. But first, the missile has to be fired manually, and locked onto target manually. Therein lies the problem.

Because of this requirement for manual operation, there has to be continual testing of the firing circuit. This is called a squib test.

These tests are done remotely from the internal fire control van. That means there is both direct wireless and cabled computerized contact and messaging to the bird's hot spot. That is the weapon's weakest link.

If they can break into that digital link, then they can take control of the bird from us. And we know that they have successfully done so in three instances.

One occurred at a site located on Okinawa, while the crews were actually in the pits pulling routine maintenance on the bird. There is not yet a clear understanding of how, but someway two messages were sent from someplace other than the internal fire control van.

The first one armed the weapon and the second launched the missile. The crew was incinerated by the exhaust blast as the missile launched.

The official explanation was that one of the cables connecting the Internal Fire Control to the Fire Control area of the missile had become frayed and was lying in a puddle of water left on the concrete floor of the silo while the crew was pulling maintenance.

The question then is why the squib tests were being run while the crew was in the pit and how did that test message get past the fire control officer, who needed to validate it before it could arm the warhead or launch the missile," Groves paused to be sure J.B. understood what he was saying.

Then he continued, "We were able to override the automatic flight center, disarm the warhead, and drop the bird into the sea. It was carrying a nuke.

The second event also involved a bird carrying a nuke. That was in Florida. The missile was in the silo, the silo was open, and the bird was raised in launch position.

No squib tests were being run. Still, the dormant missile was armed and launched. Fire control radar dropped it on the beach, and the warhead skipped across the water like a giant stone. Scary, is it not?" Groves asked and then continued.

"The third *'accidental discharge'* occurred at Ft. George G. Meade, where the National Security Agency headquarters is located. The silo was open, and the bird was raised.

A message, from an unknown source, armed and launched it. Again, we shut it down and dropped it before harm could be done. That bird was armed with a conventional warhead.

There are only two plausible explanations. The first one is that there were errors on the part of our personnel, or in the alternative, someone was able to break the codes and fire the missiles. We changed all the codes and increased the step-by-step procedural oversight but we know the security of the weapon remains at risk.

Just think of the possibilities. They can't get past our line of defense with their bombers, so they break our codes and use our weapons to hit major population centers. Now, do you understand why we need to stop the flow of information and bring this guy back?" Groves said and sat back.

"Yes sir, I do. Thank you for explaining it. I know you stretched the need to know by allowing me to ask these questions and by being so open in discussing the whys and wherefores of this mission and I appreciate it.

We will bring him out if at all possible. If not, we will be sure the flow of information stops, right there on the Big Island.

But if you will allow me one more liberty, sir? I've been thinking this over, and I believe we need to take him on Diomede rather than Alyatki.

The distance directly impacts our chances of getting him out. We can make it if we have no more than two miles to fly. But not if we have to fly fifty-eight miles.

They will scramble their jets and burn us. So, you need to push our plan to take him there on Big Diomede," J.B. said.

Groves smiled, nodded, and then asked, "Who do you want to go with you?"

"Is the Texas group still available?" J.B. asked.

"I thought you would want them. They are standing by at Eielson for you. One other thing, we don't leave anyone behind. That means living or dead, got it?"

J.B. nodded.

The truck turned left, and J.B. knew they had left the Richardson Highway and entered Eielson Air Force Base. In a few minutes, the truck turned again and stopped. J.B. heard heavy sliding doors being closed and then the flaps opened, and he could see they were in a hangar.

82

He jumped from the truck, followed by Groves. The Lieutenant led the way to the front of the hangar and into a large room.

J.B. recognized it as the same briefing room they had used to prepare for their last trip across the Bering.

Six men stood as they entered the room. Each wore plain unmarked battle dress utilities. There were no names, no unit designations not even the customary U.S. Army over the left breast.

J.B. faced them. He looked from man to man, examining them carefully, as they did him. There was Rafer Torres, Elmer Burtoff, Eckie Wade, Billy Gene (B.G) Wilson, Sonny Gritson, and Gale Johnes.

Like him, each man was from Texas, they were all police officers in civilian life, and they were all draftees. Good men, proven to be there when the fight started, there when it ended, and all would pull the trigger. They would do to ride with.

He nodded and stepped forward to shake each man's hand.

J.B. said, "We're going across again. This time our landing zone will be inland rather than on the coast. The flight might get hot because we have to go through the backyard of the NKVD.

We have a retrieve or kill mission. The target is a traitor. He was assigned to the five-sixty-second, and he stole top-secret material from Charlie Battery.

A couple CID Agents from Wainwright stumbled onto him, and now they are both dead. All this occurred on our watch, so that makes this our business. And one more thing, this Scrote is from Texas."

J.B. saw the flicker of shame in each man's eyes. "Before I go any further, does anybody want out?"

Gritson shifted his chew from one cheek to the other, pursed his lips, and shot a stream of tobacco juice across the floor. Wiping his chin on the back of his hand he asked, "You right sure he's a Texan."

J.B. turned to look at Groves who nodded, "Positive," he said.

"Then by God, it's our duty to kill him," Gritson said.

83

"Hold on, Sonny. Our first goal is to bring him out," Lieutenant Groves corrected him.

"Yeah, right. You going to be there, Lieutenant?" Wilson asked.

"Not this time B.G.," Groves said.

"Then leave the details to us, boss. We'll get it done," he said.

Groves winced, but said, "Sit down, and let's get started."

As they settled in, he stood in front of them. When he had their attention, he said, "As the sergeant said, you are going across again. You go in slick, just like you are.

You will carry nothing to identify you individually, or collectively, as members of the United States Army. That means you will not wear your dog tags, you will not carry your identification cards, and you will check your clothing to ensure there are no laundry marks.

You will not carry wallets, paper money, or change in your pockets. You will not wear watches, rings or other jewelry. You will not carry any weapon or ammunition that has not been issued specifically for this operation. Is that clear?"

After ensuring that each man understood, Groves asked, "Have any of you married or shacked up with the same women more than three days, sequentially or in the aggregate?"

Each man shook his head no.

"You know you are not to have tattoos, but since you are Texans, I better ask. Have any of you received a tattoo since we last saw you?"

Again, each man shook his head no.

" You will be operating outside the United States. You will be on the soil of another, sovereign, nation. You will not be recognized as combatants nor granted the protection of the Geneva Convention should you be captured.

Your records will not reflect your service except to list you as overseas returnee at your ETS. You will not receive hostile fire pay nor will you be decorated for any action or actions while deployed outside the United States

84

on this mission.

But, if necessary we will bring you back and bury you. I promise you will not be left behind. Are there any questions to this point?" he asked.

"You are answerable to Sergeant Gideon and him alone. From the time you leave our air space until the time you return to the same, you are his. If there is a problem, I expect him to solve it. There will be no explanation required. Are you all tracking with me here?" All nodded yes.

"You go soon, probably tomorrow night," Groves said.

A collective sigh escaped, but no one said anything. They knew they were nine-one-one for USARAL, and their number had just been dialed.

"Let's get to it," J.B. said.

Groves moved to the board, lifted the cover and picked up a pointer. The map on the board showed Alaska, the Bering Strait, and Russia. In the middle of the strait separating the superpowers were two islands, Little Diomede and Big Diomede.

Two and one-half miles inland of the big island's coast was the Siberian Counter Intelligence Station.

North of the Arctic Circle was Katzebue Sound. South and west of that was the Russian port settlement of Alyatki.

Alyatki was the headquarters of the NKVD Border Police responsible for the security of Big Diomede.

Groves pointed to Nome, Alaska. "There is a C-130 flying into Nome this afternoon. On it will be the regular relief for the civilian contractors assigned to the SEABEES there. You will be with them. You will be dressed like them. Mingle with, but do not talk to them as you depart the plane and enter the air shack. Drift out the back door, to the jeeps parked alongside the back wall.

"You will assemble here at G (Golf) Building at seventeen-hundred hours. Once inside you will be issued a new set of BDU's. Remember; check them twice to be sure there have no identifiers. Have your buddy recheck them.

You will also be issued your mission weapons here. Each man will carry a Browning Hi-Power Nine Millimeter. They will be the Belgium models, and

85

they will have no serial numbers.

You will get four magazines each holding thirteen rounds. When you load, put one in the chamber and remember to replace the one from the magazine. That gives you fourteen rounds ready to go.

Your long gun will be the M-Fourteen EBR rather than the M-Sixteen. Each of you will have twenty magazines loaded with a hotter, but smaller version of the standard issued round. Who is your Squad's Designated Marksman?" Groves asked.

"That will be Johnes, sir, and we call him Shooter," J.B. replied

"Okay, Shooter, you will draw the heavier standard weapon. It will be equipped with the longer barrel and a night vision scope. You will be issued the heavier seven point six two-millimeter round.

I am sorry about the extra weight, but your goal here should be to keep any chasers from closing on the team for as long as possible.

Also, if you do become engaged, look for the commander and waste him," the Lieutenant paused and then said, "Sergeant, put together a list of the other weaponry you want, and I will see that you have it."

J.B. said, "Thanks, boss. I know this is unusual, but I want some Claymores, fragmentation grenades, and an M-seventy-nine grenade launcher."

Groves looked surprised and asked, "What for? You know you cannot stand and fight. How will the claymores and grenades help you?"

"I suspect they will move our target in light vehicles, but there is always the possibility that they will have some armor. I can set the claymores to sweep the ambush site, penetrate and disable the vehicles and at the same time, daisy chain them to establish a kill zone should there be more of them than we expect.

Grenades with a launcher are helpful in a running fight and when you want to slow the chasers down some," J.B. said.

Groves thought a minute and said, "Okay, you got it."

"Anything else," he asked.

Burtoff asked, "Why the smaller round boss?"

86

Groves said, "The bullet weighs less than the standard round and has less muzzle velocity, but it remains supersonic longer than the bigger round. It will still be supersonic at nine-hundred and fifty yards giving you more impact damage on soft tissue and provide better penetration should you have to engage a hard target.

Your max range with this round will be twelve-hundred yards, but your surest kill zone is limited to a thousand and fifty yards. Speed kills, and you will be touching the target at twenty-eight-hundred feet per second at the nine-hundred and fifty yard to one thousand and fifty-yard mark.

And, you will be able to carry more of the rounds because of the decrease in weight. You will be going in with each man carrying four hundred rounds.

Most Soviet units will be carrying two hundred and eight rounds because they still use the larger load and can't bear the extra weight. The difference in the number of shots will be vital if you get in a firefight where you have no chance of support. Are there any other questions?" Grooves asked.

"No, okay let's move on. When you are ready to go, a slick will lift off for Little Diomede.

They will go in squawking, circle the island and set down. The watchers on Big Diomede will have them logged in and will be waiting to see what they do.

At twenty-three hundred hours, you will chopper in on a second slick. You will come into your staging area low, fast and completely blacked out. Hopefully, the watchers will not pick it up.

Then at zero two-hundred hours, the first slick will lift off again going loud and proud. They will fly the line north toward Katzebue Sound. The watchers will log them off the little island and figure them for a routine border flight.

You will lift off once the watchers are locked onto the first chopper. Your slick will be blacked out, and flying at wave-top level. You will circle to the north and come inland just off the north shore of Big Diomede.

We believe you will be undetected and the LZ will be cold. You will move out to intercept the convoy, kill the escort, grab our man and run for the southwest shore. Sergeant Gideon will activate the tracker for your extraction, and we will bring you home."

Groves paused and allowed his gaze to linger on these Arctic Warriors. *'Warriors in every sense of the word,'* he thought. *'How many of them will be alive when this is over?'* he wondered.

Pushing his thoughts aside he turned back to the board, lifted another drape to expose a picture of the target. "This is your mission target. His name is Jake Tolbert. He is a Specialist Five, recently reduced from a Spec. Six, trained on the scope in the internal fire control van.

He has been with the Five-sixty-second ADA at Charlie Battery for fifteen months. He was due for rotation in March. We aren't sure why he did this. That's up to the spooks to find out. Our job is to bring him home or to prevent him from doing any more damage.

That finishes my part. I pray God's blessings on each of you. I know the possibilities that face you. I wish I could let you could have some time with a chaplain, but you know I can't.

Go do your job, and do so knowing it is necessary. I look forward to seeing you on the other side of this mission. Sergeant, take over," Groves said. He turned and walked out of the room without looking back.

J.B. stood and faced his Texans. "I said it before, and I say it again, this one will be hot. Our only chance is to get in without them knowing we are there until we strike. Assuming we can do that, we have a chance. We have no time to waste."

We believe the target to be at Alyatki, in the custody of the KGB. They will turn him over to the GRU who will move him to their intelligence center on Big Diomede, where they will have a better chance of jamming our communications or hacking the wireless link with the missiles control module. Their intelligence center is heavily defended so we must take him before they get inside.

Our information is that they will move him on the ground to avoid the possibility of our taking him out with our SAM's on the little island. We must be on the ground before he leaves Alyatki. We will set the ambush and take care of business. We then run west to the extraction point. Do you have questions?" the sergeant paused and waited.

"I have a couple boss. Why don't the KGB put him on a chopper and fly him to center and then, how will you know when he is moving and what route he will take?" Wade asked.

"The satellite has them on a grid. Once they see the escort team move out of the KGB compound on Alyatki, they will notify our command, and we will get the word to go.

They won't fly him because we they worry about a shoot down. As to the route, we don't care because at the end of the day there is only one way into the center and we are going to be there waiting. One last thing," J.B. said, looking at the Texans. "None of us gets taken, and lives. If I'm on my feet, I'll make the shot, if not Sonny will. The progression of command will follow our pattern, same as last time. Anybody want to say anything?"

The Texans stood silently, finally Wade spoke "Yep. I got something to say. If you have to burn me boss, I want you to know it's what I wanted. Just make it clean and don't mess up my face. I want an open casket with all them gals wailing over my handsome self."

J.B. grimaced and said, "Count on it Lyn and if by chance they capture me, then whoever takes the killing shot, know I feel the same. Is there anything else?"

No one spoke, and J.B. said, "Remember this, there will be blood in the snow. Make it theirs. Let's go draw our gear," J.B. stood and led the way.

Chapter 8

The Cold LZ

J.B. knew the lift-off had to be timed perfectly. The slick would not sit down until twenty-three-hundred hours, and they could not be on station before it arrived. A squad of men standing around in fifty-five below zero weather would get attention. Attention was the last thing this operation needed.

He walked the distance from G-Building to the pickup site that afternoon and found he could do it in eight minutes. He decided to add two minutes for a margin of error.

At twenty-two-fifty he led his Texans out, and they moved in formation with weapons slung, barrels down. They were relaxed and walked with an easy stride.

Five minutes out of the building a roving guard, in an enclosed Jeep, approached them. The driver slowed, and seemed about to stop. J.B. raised his hand, then shaking his head no, waved the driver on. J.B. could see the driver's recognition that this was something he did not want to know about. He mouthed the words, *"Go With God"*, and drove on.

As the Texans stepped onto the tarmac, they heard the inbound slick. They looked to the east and watched as it came in, swung to face them, and hovered in place. The doors slid back, and the crew chief looked them over. Satisfied, he waved them onboard.

J.B. was the last man to enter the aircraft. He had not sat down before the chopper was up, and over the Strait.

The crew chief handed J.B. a headset that made it possible for J.B. to communicate with the pilot.

"Carl," came the challenge.

"Perkins" J.B. gave the counter.

"Welcome aboard, Mr. Perkins. Your target is moving, and your mission is a go. We will maintain radio silence after we close this loop.

Look out the left side of the aircraft, and you will see the decoy chopper is up with all lights on. They are making a lot of radio transmissions. You can bet the Soviets are focused on them.

I have our aircraft flying at maximum speed, and our route is parallel with the shore line, skimming the waves. Keep your squad still. There is no room for error, and I don't want the ship rocking. We will be at your landing zone in forty minutes.

Once I make the turn, we are committed, and will fly directly across the Strait. When we reach the LZ, I will flare the ship, the chief will open the doors, and your team has forty-five seconds to evacuate the aircraft. At the end of that time, we are gone. Any man still in the bay goes with us or jumps for it. That is the plan, and it does not matter if the landing zone is hot or cold. Got it?"

"Roger that sir," J.B. clicked off and handed the headset back to the chief.

'We're inbound, crossing over again. Hope this is my last time,' J.B. thought as he turned back to the bay and sat down.

The team was sleeping. J.B. smiled and thought, *'get all the sleep you can because you will need it before this is over.'* He leaned back against the seat and was instantly asleep.

J.B. lifted his head and opened his eyes as the slick slowed, and banked left. The closed doors and studded floor were covered in streaks of frost, laid on by the ships dash through the frigid arctic air.

He knew the temperature on the LZ would be below zero and that the crew chief would wait until the last possible second before opening the doors. He and his team would then exit the aircraft, weighed down by the sixty-pound packs strapped to their backs over the arctic survival suits they wore.

Another air assault made ugly by the challenging environment into which they were entering.

The nose of the Huey dropped, and then lifted a bit as the pilot flared the ship. Everything became a blur as the chief slammed the doors back and the Texans jumped into the night. On the ground, they pushed to the outer ring of the landing zone and set up fire lanes.

They scanned the tree line surrounding them looking for any movement, waiting for that first pop. Nothing, their insertion was not opposed.

J.B. called the squad together. Now they were alone in a frozen and hostile land; trespassers, come to kill or retrieve a traitor. Either way, the flow of information he was giving the enemy had to be stopped.

Looking around, J.B. thought, 'Their forest is no different than ours. But for me and mine, this one is filled with danger.'

Shaking his head, he broke off his thoughts and prepared to move the squad out.

"Check your weapons. Be sure the magazine is locked in tight, keep one round in the chamber, and put the weapon on safe. Williams, Torres, and Burtoff set yours on rock and roll. If we are engaged, I want your first magazine to be a heavy suppression fire. The rest of us will be looking for individual targets. B.G. you take the point and move us out. Let's get this done and go home," J.B. said.

The snowpack under the trees was no more than four inches deep and frozen solid by the sub-zero temperatures. B.G. checked his compass, coordinating with the stars above. J.B. was watching him and could see that he had their position confirmed as he moved forward, leading them at a quick pace.

The quiet of the forest was broken only by the sound of their boots crunching on the frozen snow. Each man had slung his weapon and placed their hands inside the mittens. Their masks were already frosted by their breath below the nose and around the mouth openings. J.B. felt the first trickle of sweat run down his spine, as testimony to the pace B.G. was setting, and the efficiency of the arctic suits they wore.

B.G. did not pause nor slow for the first forty-five minutes. Then he held up his right hand, opened it and then lowered it, palm facing down. The Texans moved out of the single file they had maintained into a double column with three yards between each man. They dropped to one knee and set their fire lanes.

B.G moved to the side of a large thicket, now barren of leaves and coated with wisps of snow driven into and through it by the winter winds. He dropped to one knee and opened his parka to retrieve his map.

J.B. checked his squad's formation. All but B.G. had their weapons unslung with their gun hands out of the mitten and on the weapon. The men faced out, weapons at the ready.

The last man of each column was facing to the rear, one covering the right flank and the other the left.

Satisfied, J.B. moved up to where B.G. was checking the map. B.G. pointed, on the map, to the site that was their first choice for the ambush. It was a bridge over a frozen stream, half a klick from the front gate of the Siberian Intelligence Center.

J.B. had picked this site after studying satellite pictures of the area. The troops stationed there had cut a three-hundred-yard field of fire out of the forest surrounding the Center. The chosen ambush site offered the last cover before that cleared area began. And, it was outside the regular patrol route of the Center's guard force.

J.B. knew that B.G. was telling him that the bridge was less than a klick straight in front of them. That meant the roadway leading to the front gate of the Center would be on a ninety-degree path north and no more than 1,000 feet ahead.

The road curved back, to loop around an outcropping of stones pushed up through the fault lines crisscrossing this island. He wanted those stones at their back in case they had to retreat. At least they would have a decent fighting position. Not that it mattered; any prolonged action and they would be overrun.

B.G. tapped him on the shoulder, breaking into his thoughts. J.B. looked up to see B.G. hold up one finger and fold it in half. He then pointed straight ahead. J.B. nodded. They had to be ready for engagement within one and a half hours. Time was an issue.

J.B. looked at the moon. It was hard to gauge the time in this darkness of the Siberian winter. Their intelligence indicated the escort would arrive at the ambush site between zero six-hundred and zero eight-hundred hours. The information was that the escort would be running light and quiet to avoid attracting attention.

J.B. figured they would have the target in an unarmored staff vehicle with one jeep leading the way and one following. He did not expect mounted weapons or more than six men with an officer and a noncom leading them. They should have light infantry weapons.

J.B. knew the escort would understand that once they left the forest and crossed the bridge, they would be moving into a cleared field of fire and under the protection of the guns from the center. They would start to relax their vigilance. Once they had the target inside the walls of the center, he would be as untouchable as he had been in the KGB compound at Alyatki.

J.B. looked up again. It was time to move. Looking back along the column he gave the thumbs up then with an open hand he waved them to their feet. He stood and waved B.G. back into the column and then took the point leading the squad forward.

J.B. set a quick pace, and soon saw the bridge ahead. He swung the column into the tree line to keep their tracks out of sight as much as possible. They entered the frozen stream bed two hundred yards west of the bridge and moved east.

Fifty yards from the bridge, they climbed out of the creek bed and up the bank. J.B. pointed to a cluster of giant pine trees on either side of the bridge, where the road curved at the end of the last approach to the bridge. He nodded at Torres and Burtoff.

The two men moved to the trees. J.B. watched as they removed four of the claymores from the weapons sack. They mounted them three feet up from the ground on the trees and then daisy chained them for maximum impact.

'Those claymores are not well hidden. But I have to take the chance. If the Soviets show up in jeeps, I can stop them with rifle fire. But if they show up in armored vehicles I will need the Claymores to stop them. I will wait until the lead jeep has crossed the bridge, the staff car should be on the bridge, and as the trail jeep passes the first tree, we will hit them.

Wade and Wilson will hit the lead jeep, hosing them down on full auto. Burtoff and Torres will take the trailing jeep.

The claymores will be our ace in the hole. Wade will detonate them only if the escorting troops are in armored vehicles or if there are more troops than we expect, and a firefight erupts.

We have the claymores positioned high enough on the tree to leave a two feet high safe zone. That will allow my squad to hit the ground and cover up until the fire zone is clear.

Two thousand eight hundred three-point two-millimeter steel balls packed on a charge of C-4 explosive will be propelled out into the kill zone. Each traveling at three thousand nine hundred and thirty-seven feet per second. They will sweep away everything in a sixty-degree arc fifty-five yards wide.

Gritson and I will be waiting under the bridge. Once the firing stops or the Claymores have done their work, we will exit our cover and storm the staff car. We will go with pistols in hand for this close-range work, kill any surviving escorts and secure the target, if he is still alive.

If I fall, Gritson will kill Tolbert. He will take charge of the squad, harvest what hard intelligence he can, if the target is dead he will cut a thumb off to prove his identity, and lead the squad out of the ambush site and run for the sea.

Johnes will be responsible for covering the squad with the scoped weapon during the operation. Should things go to hell and the troops from the Center join the fight, he will provide covering fire until the squad could develop a fighting position,' J.B. sifted through the plan.

Finally, J.B. was satisfied that he had done all he could. He became aware that the wind had increased. Pulling his parka hood over his head, he glanced to the west where he saw dark clouds heavy with snow. *'If that storm hits before we spring the ambush, things are going to get dicey,'* he thought.

The reduced visibility would make it harder for the escort to detect the ambush, but it would also make the Texans' selection of targets harder and decrease their mobility in running for the extraction point. He knew the slick would be there for them but sensed this was not going to be as fluid an operation as he had hoped. He checked his Texans and settled in under the bridge to wait.

Chapter 9

Death and Reflection

"Drive toward Eielson," Mayfield told Box.

"That's a military installation," Nikita said.

"It's federal, and we're federal," Mayfield replied.

"Where are we going from there," Nikita asked.

Mayfield ignored her and asked Box, "Did you search both of them before putting them in the car?"

Box shook his head no.

Nikita laughed. "Oh, I see. You think I might have some listening device or maybe a tracker planted on my person. Is that it, are my people going to run you off the road and rescue me, or will they be waiting for me at whatever destination you have in mind?"

Mayfield and Box looked straight ahead and said nothing.

Nikita said, "Demetrio is bleeding again. He is fading in and out, and I fear that Jake smashing him in the face with that lamp may have given him a concussion. He needs a doctor."

Mayfield turned to look at Demetrio. What he saw alarmed him. "Pull over up here when you can," he directed Box.

Box found a wide spot and pulled the car from the roadway and onto the graveled shoulder. Mayfield stepped from the car and walked around to the back. He opened the door, leaned in and saw that Demetrio had his head tilted back resting on the top of the seat cushion.

Demetrio seemed to be struggling for air. Blood was bubbling from his broken nose, and Mayfield thought some might be blocking his nasal passages. The nose itself was totally crushed, one eye socket appeared to be fractured, and both eyes were swollen horribly.

Mayfield called to Demetrio, "Demetrio, Demetrio. Can you hear me?"

There was no reaction. Mayfield lifted one of Demetrio's eyelids and saw that the eye was dilated and not reactive to the light. He looked at Nikita. "Speak to him in your language."

Nikita shook her head and said, "It will do no good. He is not conscious. He is dying. He may be the lucky one."

Mayfield closed the door. He walked to the front and sat down. "Get us to Eielson," he said.

Box pulled into traffic and sped toward the airbase. Mayfield picked up the radio and said, "Fairbanks forty-four to Fairbanks Station. "

"Fairbanks Station, go ahead forty-four," came the reply.

"Contact the control at our destination and request a physician meet us on arrival. Inform the boss that one of our packages appears to be a signal twenty-seven."

"Roger that, Fairbanks forty-four. Standby," was the reply.

Box turned from the Richardson Highway and approached the front gate. The Air Force Security Police Officer on duty stepped from the guard station and held up his hand for the vehicle to stop. Box rolled down his window as the young officer stepped up.

"Good morning gentlemen. How can I help you?" the officer asked.

Mayfield leaned across Box and showing his credential said, "Special Agent Mayfield from Fairbanks F.B.I. I believe you have been informed of our arrival."

"Fairbanks forty-four," the radio broke in.

The officer looked at the radio as Mayfield lifted the microphone, "Go ahead Fairbanks Station."

"Your host has been informed, and the physician is on station waiting for your arrival."

"Roger, Fairbanks station. Be advised we are at the front gate now."

The Security Police officer looked at Demetrio, "Is that the twenty-seven sir?"

Mayfield nodded his head, sighed and said, "I'm afraid he's going to be if I don't get him to a doctor, soon."

A jeep approached with red lights flashing, and the officer said, "Follow him, sir."

The jeep drove away, and Box swung the sedan in behind him. They raced across the base and into a hangar on the flight line.

Mayfield jumped from the car and ran around to open the back door. He pointed to Nikita and said, "Box, keep your hands on her. Do not let go of her for any reason."

Box hustled around the car and pulled Nikita from the back seat. He looped his left hand over and through the links on her handcuffs and pulled her back against him.

Mayfield asked, "Where is the doctor?"

"Right here." a man in medical scrubs stepped through the door and into the hanger. He walked to the car and leaned into the back seat. He lifted Demetrio's eyelid, checked his wrist, then his neck for a pulse and then pulled his stethoscope from his pocket. He listened for a minute moving the instrument around on Demetrio's chest.

The doctor said, "He's in a coma. The airway is restricted by the compression of the crushed cartilage of the nose. The bigger problem is, and I would need some pictures to be sure, but it appears that the bone at the top of his nose was broken loose by the force of the blow involved in this trauma.

The possibility is that it has pierced the frontal lobe of his brain. The brain is bleeding. That accounts for the coma. He needs surgery right away, or he will die."

Mayfield rubbed his face and looked at Box. "Where is our plane," he asked.

"Out front sir," an airman said, pointing to a C-130 sitting on the tarmac with the ramp down.

"Help me get him on board," Mayfield said to the airman.

"You will kill him if you put him on that plane," the doctor said.

"Stand aside, doctor. We appreciate your help. There will be no record of this visit," Mayfield said.

"I know," the doctor said as he walked away.

The airman called two of his buddies. They put Demetrio in a wheeled office chair and pushed him out to the plane. They picked him up in a fireman's carry and lugged him up the ramp and sat him down on the canvas bench. They buckled him in, draped a blanket over his legs and walked away.

Box led Nikita up the ramp. "This is going to be a long flight. I'm taking the handcuffs off for your comfort, but they go right back on if you give us any trouble. Understand?"

"I understand. You won't have any trouble. For me it's over," she said. "But I do need to use the bathroom before we get started."

Box looked at the crew chief. The Chief pointed to a door at the front of the bay and said, "The restroom is there little lady."

Box walked her to the door and held it open. "What's with you Americans? Do you all like to watch girls pee?"

Box said nothing. Nikita sighed and sat down. When she had finished, he led her to the bench and buckled her in. The crew chief handed her a couple of blankets.

"Thank you for giving me two, how about giving another one to Demetrio?" she asked.

The chief shook his head and said, "Lady, he's not going to need the one he has for very long."

Box and Mayfield sat down and strapped in. The chief raised the ramp, picked up his intercom and spoke into it, "Our load is secure, and the ramp is up and locked. We're ready to go back here, sir."

The engines increased their whine, and the plane began its taxi. In a matter of minutes, they were airborne. The chief stood up, looked around, and said, "See you gents just before touchdown." With that, he stepped from the bay onto the flight deck and closed the door.

The plane climbed to clear the mountain ranges that they would encounter as they winged their way south. The temperature inside the bay dropped, making the blankets most welcome.

Nikita pulled her blankets up to her chin and looked at Demetrio. His head was slumped forward, and his body sagged against the chest straps. She knew he was dead.

She looked at Mayfield, and he just stared back. Nikita choked down a sob and leaned back, turning her head, so she did not have to look Mayfield in the eye. 'His eyes are as dead as Demetrio's,' she thought as she drifted off to sleep.

The change of the engine pitch woke her. She could tell they were in the landing approach.

The wheels touched down with a screech, and the plane rolled out its' taxi. She could not see outside the plane, but she could tell they were turning. She rocked back and forth a couple of times with the motion of the plane as it lurched to its berth and then the engines were cut.

They had arrived. The next step in her life of isolation was about to begin. She stood, and Mayfield snapped the cuffs back on her. "That's not necessary. I mean, where am I going?"

"You have killed two of us already. I don't want to be the third," he answered her.

Nikita smiled and walked forward in reaction to his slight pressure on her left elbow. The sun was bright, and she blinked as they walked down the ramp.

"Welcome to Peterson Air Force Base sir," a member of the ground crew said.

"Thank you, sergeant," Mayfield replied. "Is our car here?"

"Yes, sir. Follow me," the sergeant said.

He led them to a black Chevrolet Suburban. Nikita noticed that only the windshield was clear. The remaining windows were blacked out.

Mayfield opened the back door and told her to step up and in. She placed her hands on the rail above the doorframe and pulled herself up and sat down on the leather seats. Box slid in on the other side, reached across and fastened her seat belt.

She was surprised that she could see out of the same windows that prevented her from seeing in. She watched as they pulled Demetrio from the plane and carried him to the back of the Suburban.

The doors opened, and they rolled his body inside. The sergeant dropped a blanket over him, slammed the doors and slapped his hand on the back glass.

The Suburban pulled away from the flight line and headed to the front gate. Mayfield asked the driver, "Where are we going?"

The driver looked in the mirror at Nikita and said, "Cheyenne Mountain, inside range."

Nikita shuddered. *'How did this get so messed up? Demetrio is dead, and my future is one of isolation, locked away inside America, where freedom is supposed to reign,'* she sighed.

She looked out the window as the suburban rolled along. She was mesmerized by her reflection. Hard unblinking eyes, framed by a painted face, stared at her. They pulled her downward, into her past.

The reflections carried her back to her childhood home, if you could call the one-room walk-up in central Moscow a home.

The place reeked of cabbage, fish, and tobacco left by former occupants. The concrete floors were covered in soiled cotton rugs, and the paint had peeled from the walls long ago.

There were two beds pushed against the walls on opposite sides of the small space, one for her, and one for her mother, and whatever man she had taken in at the instant. A stove, a sink, and a table were pushed against the far wall.

The flat had no toilet. There was a communal one for the residents on each floor of the building. Their apartment shared a thin wall with the facility for their floor, adding to the sounds and smells of her life at home.

Her mother stretched a string of twine, from which she hung a sheet, between the beds. It was a feeble attempt to shield Nikita from the immodest activities of the adults.

It hid little, and Nikita made a habit of leaving the apartment to distance herself from the sights and sounds of her mother entertaining the men.

She knew that her mother took men into her bed to provide for herself and her daughter. Knowing this did not ease the pain, erase the shame, or quiet the revulsion of watching the violence visited on her mother by those who used and then beat her.

The men began to stare at her, and she knew that it was only a matter of time until she became her mother. She accepted this as a woman's lot but determined to change her circumstances.

She was painfully thin, but beautiful. Her beauty attracted men and boys. She soon learned that the boys could provide little and expected much in return. The men also came with an expectation but were able to entertain her in the best tearooms, restaurants, and bars of the city. By the age of sixteen, she had dropped all pretenses of childhood and adopted the life of a woman of the night. Her self-prophecy was fulfilled. She became her mother.

She met an older man in a tearoom, just off Red Square. After a frank conversation in which he told Nikita what he expected of her, she became his mistress. He provided her with an apartment, a cash allowance and an assurance of privilege. He demanded little, and it was not unusual for several months to pass between his visits.

His name was Karl, and he worked in the Kremlin. Nikita did not know what position or rank he held, but she was fascinated by the fact that he was always accompanied by bodyguards, who would wait in the hallway outside the apartment while he visited Nikita.

Karl told Nikita he had commissioned a background search on her and her family line. She was interested to hear him say she was of pure ethnic Russian stock.

Karl's words echoed in her mind even now, *"Your blood is that of Mother Russia. It is in you and those like you that the worker and the czar will become one. You and your kind will one day bury the weak while uniting the workers in taking their rightful place as rulers of all the world."*

She had been so young, and so filled with the visions espoused by Karl. She knew now that it had all been part of the plan to recruit her, first into the party and then into the security services. She had no education, no intellectual skills but she had her youth and her beauty.

102

Would she be willing to give that which she had to further the cause of the party and Mother Russia? The question had been put to her over tea after a lavish dinner in a restaurant adjacent to Red Square. Her answer had been an emphatic, yes!

Next came two years of training by the KGB in their basement rooms beneath the Kremlin. Then had come field assignments, within the Union, in which she provided evidence of dissent or behaviors the KGB considered treasonous.

The targets of her assignments were ordinary citizens at first, and then as she grew more proficient, she was working governmental officials that the Kremlin wanted to be removed from office. She would watch as the raiding teams hauled the targets from their homes, usually in the middle of the night. Most of them disappeared never to be heard of again.

Her first kill came next. The target was a journalist who insisted, despite warnings, to continue his investigation of corruption within the Congress of Soviets. It was so simple. She waited in the hallway outside his office and shot him as he left for the day. She dropped the silenced pistol in the nearest trash can, walked to the elevator and left the building.

Then she was sent outside of the Union for the first time, to America. She was assigned to work the military personnel frequenting the bars around Fort Meade Maryland. Her purpose was to obtain as much information as she could about the missile defenses protecting the East Coast Military District.

The information she provided resulted in the arming and launching one of the missiles while it sat in the silo. The Americans initiated an investigation of the event.

One of the soldiers who frequented Nikita's apartment tipped her that another of her regular customers had given the investigators her name. Her managers feared the investigators would arrest her, so they immediately moved her across the country to Alaska.

In Alaska, she was once again assigned to glean information from the soldiers attached to the missile defenses in that area. She had been installed in the Polaris Hotel, met Jake and now here she sat, in this Suburban speeding toward an American prison where she would likely spend the rest of her life.

She had come far, but she was still her mother. She felt the hot tears spill out of her eyes and run down her face dripping from her chin onto her chest.

She glanced down to see the damp spots on the cloth covering the swell of her breasts. Karl had called them her best asset, that to which men were first drawn when meeting her. And now they were soaked in the bitterness and pain known only by women, who were used by men.

Chapter 10

Sleep Walking

Jake was running through a dark tunnel along a path choked with vines slapping at his face, tripping over roots that sprang up out of the ground to block his way. He saw light filtering through the darkness ahead and turned to it with a renewed burst of energy. He raced to be free of this oppressive jungle that seemed to be pressing ever closer, seeking to lock him within a cell of carnivorous vines.

"Wake up. We must go. Get up and get dressed." Jake could hear the voice and felt a hand on his shoulder shaking him. He rolled away from the hand and pulled a pillow over his head to block out the sound.

The covers were stripped from him, and rough hands pulled him from the bed onto the floor. "Get up, now!" the voice demanded.

Jake opened his eyes to see a blurry figure swaying over him. He rubbed his eyes to clear his vision and mumbled, "I must go now?"

"Yes, now. Here are your clothes. We have ten minutes to get you dressed and downstairs. You leave today." Jake recognized the face of Janyke.

Jake struggled to his feet and sat on the edge of the bed. Janyke tossed his trousers to him. Jake stood and stepped into them. He put on a shirt, socks, and shoes and was pushed out the door and down the stairs. Jake stumbled and thought, *'am I awake, is this happening or am I sleepwalking?'*

The woman, whose name he still did not know, stood at the front door. She handed a slim case to Janyke. "There is a passport, some cash, and tickets for the six o'clock flight to Seoul in here.

The passport, of course, is a forgery but we used his military identification photo, and that's what the ticket agent will be focused on. We will have our people steward his progress through customs in Seoul.

You will watch him board and then remain until the plane takes off. Report back to me once he is in the air or if there are problems."

She turned to Jake. "You will board a Korean Air flight from Seattle to Seoul. Once in Seoul, you will be cleared through customs by one of our people.

From there you will be taken across to Pyongyang where one of our planes will transport you to the next station. Let me warn you that you have chosen your course. Any attempt to change your mind or to escape our control will result in your death. We will kill you; please believe me."

Jake nodded, "I do believe you," he said.

Jake was amazed at how easy it had been. No questions at Sea-Tag, an uneventful flight into Seoul, and straight through customs with only an icy, contemptuous stare from the customs officer.

Once clear of customs he was met by two men as he walked through the security gate. One said, "Don't look at us. Walk with us, we have a care waiting."

Jake did as told and they drove from the airport grounds onto a highway choked with traffic. "Wow, this is just like a western city," Jake said.

Neither of the men answered or looked at him. They drove out of the city and to the international bridge separating the two Korea's.

The South Korea Military Police glanced at their passports and waved them through. The North Korea Border Police glanced at the American face and spoke to the Koreans in their tongue.

They got a sharp retort in return, and the driver drove through without waiting for approval.

The escorts took Jake to a military airfield, placed him on a jet and he was flown to the prison where he now lay on a cot in a frozen cell. Jake looked around at his place of confinement.

The walls were made of rough stone set in unfinished concrete. A tiny window was cut in the wall, high above the cot he lay on. The single paned window was a sheet of ice, and the wall was covered with frost. The cold dominated the cell.

He lay still, forcing himself to endure the cold, drawing it in even as he felt the burn on his face. He hoped that the physical pain would somehow ease the anguish of his heart, the shame he felt. It was not working.

He replayed the events of the last two days over and over again in his mind. He had known that Layne, or Nikita, was using him. Why did he not have the strength to walk away? Was it because, contrary to his whole life

106

experience, he dared hope a woman like her would be interested in him, little Jake Tolbert? Jake sighed and wondered what awaited him.

He heard the sound of boots on stone, approaching his cell. Keys rattled, and the guard said, "It is your move day. You are to leave here at zero six hundred hours. Your escort will be here at zero five forty-five. If you want to eat, get up, and come here."

Jake rolled over and saw the guard setting a tray of food down on a table, outside the cell door. Steam wafted up from a cup and he wanted something to warm to drink. "Coffee?" he asked, pointing at the cup.

"No, it is tea. And there is some toast if you like," the guard said.

Jake walked to the table and wrapped his hands around the steaming mug. He lifted it, blew across the top, and took a sip. The tea was strong and sweet. Jake lifted it again and drank deeply. Setting the cup down he smacked his lips and grunted his pleasure.

The guard laughed, and slapped him on the back. Jake had taken his first bite of the toast when he heard more boots approaching.

He raised his eyes to see the guard snap to attention as a young man in uniform walked around the corner. He said something to the guard who went to parade rest.

The officer then spoke to Jake, "I am Major Kowalski. I am detailed to escort you to our Counter Intelligence Center on Big Diomede. You know of it, yes?"

Jake chewed his toast while considering his answer.

The Major moved so quickly Jake never had a chance to react. The slap across his face, knocked Jake to the floor beside the table. The hot, metallic taste of blood filled his mouth.

"Get on your feet and answer me," the Major spoke calmly but with every expectation of being obeyed.

Jake pushed himself up off the floor, pulled his shirt down, ran his tongue across his busted lips, and looked up at the Major. As he raised his head, he saw the blow coming. It hit him square in the nose, and Jake felt a searing pain.

"Do you hear well? English is your mother tongue, is it not? Do enlisted personnel in the American army not give quick answers to their officers or is there another reason for your insolent behavior?" the Major asked.

Jake answered quickly, "Sorry, sir. Yes sir, we know about the center on the big island."

"Good. Now that we understand each other, let me tell you that we will move you in my staff car. The complete detail will consist of five troops and me.

Our goal is to deliver you safely to the Center, or kill you if that is not possible. Be assured that I do not care which way it works out.

Sit quietly, except when asked to speak, do as you are told, and you will be delivered safely in five hours, give or take as you say."

The Major turned to the guard who immediately snapped to attention. "Does he have any baggage or clothing, a coat, and hat perhaps?"

"Yes, sir. He has a coat and hat on his bed. I will get it if the Major wants."

"Yes, get it and walk him out to my car."

He turned to Jake as the guard trotted into the cell for his hat and coat. "Bring your tea. Leave the toast; I don't want to listen to you chew."

Jake was at attention, "Yes, sir."

The Major smiled, '*these Americans learn quickly*,' he thought.

Jake settled into the back seat. The Major sat in front with his driver. They were led away from the prison compound by two guards in a jeep, and followed by two more in a second jeep. The convoy was tight, and Jake could tell they were going to move quickly.

Two hours brought them to the coast. A ferry was waiting, and all three vehicles drove onto it. A quick trip across the sound and they were deposited on the North-Western shore of Big Diomede Island.

The Major picked up a radio and spoke in Russian. Jake didn't understand the language but knew the message. The Major had just tightened the convoy. Jake realized that his chances of escape were quickly evaporating.

The convoy pushed on through the early morning arriving at the edge of a forest around noon. The Major called a halt and stepped from his car.

Jake watched as the Major glanced to the west, where dark storm clouds were gathering. He saw the Major turn the collar of his coat up, and pull his cap down, to keep it from blowing off of his head. Jake leaned forward and looked up at the clouds. They were speeding across the sky, pushed by a strong wind that was whistling through the tree-tops.

The Major returned to the car and told his driver to contact the Center on the secure channel.

Jake watched as the driver did as ordered and handed the radio to the Major. Major Kowalski spoke into the handset. Jake could not understand what he was saying, but it was clear from his focus on the clouds that he was concerned about entering the forest with the storm that was brewing.

After a few minutes of conversation, Jake saw the Major nod his head, heard him say "Da," and hand the radio back to the driver. He sat for a minute, sighed deeply, and waved the driver forward.

They entered the forest, and the roadway turned to a path, just wide enough to accommodate the vehicles. Jake could feel the tension increase as they pushed deeper and deeper into the forest. The tension, the lack of sleep, and the warm air flowing from the staff car's heater worked its' way, and soon Jake was asleep.

Chapter 11

The Bridge

Jake woke as the staff car stopped. The Major cursed softly, and pushed against the door held closed by the force of the wind. Jake realized that the dark skies had released a winter storm while he slept. A gust of wind rocked the car, and the Major gave up trying to get the car door open.

Jake saw the lead jeep stopped in the middle of the pathway some three-car lengths ahead of the staff car. He twisted around and looked out the back window to see the trail jeep idling about the same distance behind them. *'Good discipline,'* he thought.

Jake turned back to see the Major watching him in the rearview mirror. Jake leaned forward and asked, "Are we stranded, sir?"

"No, the wind is blowing the snow off the road, but there is a bridge just ahead, and I do not want to move closer until I can inspect the approach," the Major replied.

"I want you to sit still. Do not get out of the car. You know, that even if you were able to escape us, the cold would kill you in a matter of minutes."

'Interesting,' Jake thought, *'they see me as a prisoner rather than a defector. I wish I had known this would be their position. If my future is to be spent in captivity, the American prison would certainly have been better than what awaits me on the other side of that bridge.'* Jake nodded his agreement, "How cold is it, sir?" he asked.

The Major pointed to the thermometer in the corner of the windshield, "Minus forty-eight Celsius or for your Fahrenheit that is fifty-five degrees below zero."

The Major turned to his driver and spoke sharply. The driver opened the door on his side and stepped from the car. The Major slid across the seat and out of the car. The driver returned to the car and adjusted the rearview mirror so he could see Jake.

Jake watched as the Major pulled a mask down over his face and turned the collar of his leather officer's jacket up to protect the back of his neck from the sharp wind. He stepped out and began the trek to the front of the little convoy. The wind pushed him off stride as he moved from the protection of the staff car, but he quickly regained his balance and moved forward.

A few steps beyond the first Jeep, the Major stopped and raised his binoculars to rest on the eye openings of the facemask. Jake knew from experience that the mask would limit the clarity of his vision but was necessary to keep the cold metal frame of the glasses frame from sticking to his face.

Major Kowalski swept the glasses back and forth over the bridge, the roadway beyond the bridge, and the approach between the first Jeep and the bridge. He turned and inspected the forest on either side of the approach, and beyond the bridge. *'Something is not right. But what?'* the Major wondered.

He scanned the area on both sides and in front of the bridge again. *'Once we leave the forest and start our approach to that bridge, we will not be able to turn back. We will be in open country, and once on that bridge, we will be in a perfect ambush profile,'* he thought. He sighed, and suddenly a vision of his family back in Poland swam into his thoughts. He shivered with a chill borne of something other than this Siberian storm.

'Maybe I am being overly skittish. I see nothing amiss. The roadway is clear, and once we cross the bridge we are within two-thousand feet of the center. Inside those walls and we will be safe. But still, there is someone out there, I can feel them, but where are they,' he mumbled as he swept the area again with his glasses. He saw nothing, his shoulders slumped in resignation and he told himself, *'We go now, and we go quickly.'*

Jake could see the Major had reached his decision. He could tell he was worried and Jake could understand that. If there were to be an ambush, the curve in the road or better still the bridge itself would be a perfect place to spring it.

'That bridge is my last link with any hope of escape,' Jake reasoned. He glanced out of the corner of his eye at the driver and saw that the driver was watching him in the mirror. Jake could see that the driver was reading his mind.

The driver moved his head from side to side and lifted his right hand to reveal he was holding his pistol, cocked and ready. Jake sat back against the seat, and the driver smiled.

Jake shifted his attention to the Major and saw him striding toward the bridge. *'He's going to walk the route,'* Jake thought. But when the Major stepped from the protection of the tree line, the Siberian winter slashed at him with its untamed wind. His leather jacket provided little protection against the bone-chilling cold.

The Major turned and headed back to the shelter of the trees, pausing only to glance back over his shoulder at the bridge and then strode toward the car.

The driver chuckled, and Jake smiled. Both had wiped any semblance of levity from their face as the driver stepped out to allow the Major back into the car.

The driver sat down and watched the Major shaking from the ordeal visited on him by Mother Nature. The driver opened a thermos of tea and filled a cup for the Major.

He removed the mask from his face, grasped the cup of steaming liquid and sucked it in. The hot tea helped him stop shaking.

He pushed the frozen collar of his jacket down and out of contact with the back of his neck. He held his hands in front of the heater's blast of hot air, then gently rubbed them across his face.

Jake could see the white spots on the Major's neck. *'That's frostbite. The burning will start soon, and be followed by intense pain as the damaged nerves report the dead and dying tissue. That is the price he is going to pay for not shedding his stylish jacket for a sensible arctic parka,'* Jake thought.

The Major spoke into the radio, and the convoy moved forward. The Major lowered his eyes to find the thermos for another cup of the hot tea. The driver stopped the car and lifted the thermos from where it was resting against his leg and handed it to the Major.

As the Major poured the tea, his head tipped forward. The driver sat watching and waiting for the Major to finish pouring, before moving the car forward again.

Both had lost visual contact with the bridge and the approach. But Jake sensed something was about to happen. He kept his eyes glued to the bridge. He saw a movement inside the tree line. Jake dropped to the floor of the staff car. The Major and the driver both turned to see what Jake was doing.

Then it came, the hammering of automatic weapons fire.

Chapter 12

Melting Snow ~ Vanishing Blood

The Texans were cold. They had been sitting in the ambush position for more than an hour. J.B. watched the storm building and knew that, depending on its severity, it could push them to find a place with better shelter. It would be a matter of survival, not comfort.

The storm struck with a violence that only Siberia can wield. It unleashed winds that drove the chill to minus seventy-five degrees.

The multi-layered arctic suits kept the team alive and reasonably comfortable when moving, but sitting still enabled the cold to reach inside and grasp them in its' frozen hold. J.B. had decided to move into the deep forest , when the lead jeep come around the curve.

He turned to his team and confirmed that they saw the jeep also. They watched as the convoy halted and the officer walked forward inspecting the approach to the bridge.

J.B. was sure that he would see the claymores. But then the officer stepped from the tree line and was rocked back by the blast of arctic cold whipping through the open bed of the creek.

J.B. saw the officer was wearing a leather jacket rather than an arctic parka and knew his stay outside would be a relatively short one. The team relaxed as he retreated to the shelter of his staff car.

From the cover of the bridge, J.B. lifted his weapon, signaling the team to make theirs ready. The lead jeep was rolling across the bridge.

J.B. slung his rifle over his left shoulder. He removed the Browning nine-millimeter from the holster and checked to ensure there was a round in the chamber.

J.B. listened as the tires on the lead vehicle crunched slowly forward and then off the bridge. 'Now,' he thought, and the storm was split as Wade and Wilson opened fire with their M-14's.

J.B. and Gritson exited from under the bridge on opposite sides. Keeping low, they moved up the bank to their positions below the top of the roadway.

J.B. looked to his left and saw Wade and Wilson standing beside the lead jeep emptying their magazines into the occupants. The bodies jerked and bounced under the impact of the supersonic rounds ripping through skin and bone at such close range. He checked that target as finished, and moved mentally to the next.

Turning to his right, he saw Torres and Burtoff down on their knees on opposite sides of the trailing jeep. One was concentrating fire on the front and the other on the back. It was an effective crossfire that had disabled the vehicle and killed its occupants. J.B. heard himself say, *'Target number two neutralized.'*

J.B. waved to Gritson and they advanced on the staff car. The driver stepped from the car with a pistol in his hand and J.B. shot him in the forehead. The driver's body was slammed back against the open door, and then bounced forward, rolling onto his left side as he fell.

J.B. could see that the hollow point had mushroomed on its' passage into and through the brain. The forces of the explosive driven journey blew the back of the skull apart, pushing brain and bone out in a spray, covering the open door.

Gritson approached the passenger side door slowly. Peering inside he called to J.B., "They're on the floor, boss."

"Wait for me," J.B. said. "We will move up together. I will cover from this side as you open the door on that side."

They moved forward. J.B. kneeled, and swung his pistol into and through the open driver's door, as Gritson pulled open the passenger's side rear door.

J.B. saw the Soviet Officer on the floorboard of the car. The driver's blood and brains were splashed across his face. The officer raised his empty hands in surrender.

J.B. could see that he was fighting to keep from vomiting. He lost the fight, and bent forward spewing the contents of his stomach from his mouth and nose.

J.B. leaned in, placed his pistol on the top of the major's head, and pulled the trigger.

Gritson was concentrating on their target, on the back floorboards. He glanced at J.B. with a question in his eyes. J.B. shook his head no and said, "Don't kill him. Get him out of the car and search him for weapons."

Gritson opened the back door and said, "Get out of the car. Keep your hands where I can see them. Breath deep and I will waste your sorry ass where you stand."

Jake crawled from the car. "Don't shoot me," he begged. "I am an American, like you. They were holding me against my will. I want to go home."

Gritson shook his head and said, "No, you are not like us. You stopped being an American when you went over to them."

The rest of the team gathered around, and J.B. called out, "Wade, be sure those claymores are safe. We are standing in their kill zone."

He turned to Johnes and said, "Johnes, mount the roof of the staff car, and cover both ends of this site. Copy me now, Shooter. Anyone approaching us is the enemy, and is to be killed on sight!"

"Copy that boss," Johnes said as he mounted the roof of the vehicle with his weapon ready.

J.B. nodded, and said to the rest of the team, "Reload now. Be sure you have one in the chamber, with a full magazine. Put your weapons on safe."

Once satisfied that all weapons were loaded and ready, J.B. said, "Gritson, check the bodies. Put a round into each one's head to be sure they are dead. Wade and Wilson go through their pockets, and take anything that you think might be of value to the spooks.

Torres, you watch Tolbert. Smoke him if he makes a wrong move. We are out of here in five minutes, not one second more. Move," J.B. ordered.

The ambush had been simple, brutal and quick. *'Just like the LT. said it would be'* J.B. thought. Still, he was fighting a nagging feeling that it had been too easy.

J.B. figured there was a chance the roar of the Siberian force winds had drowned out the sounds of the light arms. If so, they were way ahead of this game, and had a good chance of covering a lot of ground before anyone came looking for these he had just killed.

But come they would, and he needed to prepare for them.

He moved to the claymores and disconnected the remote detonator but left the daisy chain intact. Then he ran a trip wire under the staff car and tied it off to the front bumper. He connected it to the claymores, covered it with snow and signaled to the rest of the team that the area was now hot.

Whoever came would eventually approach the staff car. If his luck held, the enemy would trip the wire, detonating the claymores, and shredding all in the kill zone. They would die a nasty death, but it should be relatively quick.

'Dead sons of the Mother Land forgotten as their blood vanished with the melting of the snow. Better theirs, than ours,' J.B. thought.

Another plus would be that the sound of the detonation would carry for miles. Hearing it would give him an idea of how much of a lead he had on his pursuers. J.B. called Johnes down off of the car.

"Tolbert, listen carefully. We are moving to our extraction point. My orders are to take you back if possible, or kill you if not. Do you understand me?"

Jake nodded his head indicating he understood and J.B. said, "Tell me where the SOP Manual is."

"Major Kowalski had it in a tin box that he loaded into the trunk, there," Jake said, pointing to the staff car. "But they made several copies of it before we left."

"Get it, Wade. Remember that zone is hot. Stay behind the car and step light," J.B. ordered.

Wade grimaced, but moved forward, opened the trunk, and pulled the tin box from the car. "This damned thing is heavy, boss. Are we going to hump it to the extraction point? The traitor said they have copies, so why not just leave it here? " Wade asked.

"No way," J.B. said. "It is ours, and it goes with us. Open the box, get our stuff, and anything else that you think the spooks would want."

Wade opened the box, pulled the SOP Manual and several other folder sized envelopes out. He dispersed them among the team members.

"Wade, I want you to take the lead. Point us due west, and keep us moving. If we are intercepted our best hope is to fight our way through. If we stop to fight, we will be overrun.

117

Tolbert, I hope you can keep up. Do your best because I will not allow you to slow us down. Do you have any questions? No, move out then." J.B. said.

Wade moved to the tree line, disappearing as the forest swallowed him. The team followed. J.B. was the last in.

He stopped inside the cover of the trees, and looked back to survey the ambush site. *'The wind has covered our tracks with snow. That is the good news. The bad, he had not accounted for the roar of the wind as it passed through the pine trees. That will make it hard to hear the claymores when they are tripped,* J.B. thought.

He was about to turn to follow the team when he caught sight of movement in the trees opposite the far end of the bridge. He slid back into the thick underbrush, and dropped to one knee.

J.B.'s heart was thumping against his chest. *'I saw movement, I know I did. But where is it now?'* J.B. asked himself.

He slowed his breathing, and forced himself to scan the area by moving only his eyes back and forth, up and down, dividing the space into zones of observation.

'There they are,' J.B. could see the shapes of men on their knees beside the tree trunks and on their bellies in the snow under the brush.

One had field glasses and was sweeping them back and forth over the ambush site.

J.B. could do nothing but sit and watch. Any move he made would be seen. *'Here they come,'* J.B. mouthed as he watched the soldiers approach the smoking vehicles.

J.B. could see that they were tense. He watched as they withdrew their gloved hands from their arctic mittens, clicked the safeties off, and moved forward.

He admired the way they were moving. They swiveled their heads back and forth, making sure the path was clear. *'These are well-trained men who know how to advance into a killing zone,'* J.B. thought.

Their leader stopped them about fifteen feet from the first jeep. He waved three men forward, pointing to the jeep.

J.B. watched as the three fanned out with six yards separating them. They moved together, communicating with each other by a glance, a nod or a gesture toward a given point of interest. They covered the distance, checking the road where patches of blown snow could conceal a trip wire or mine. *'Good troops,'* he found himself thinking.

Satisfied that the area was safe, they moved to the jeep, and looked inside. J.B. knew the sight would sicken, and enrage them. One turned, and waved his comrades forward.

The rest of the squad moved quickly to the jeep, placing their feet in the tracks of those who had gone before them. J.B. could hear them as they vented their anger. He could see the determination for revenge on their faces as they turned to survey the trees around the scene.

The squad leader waved the same three toward the staff car. They stepped out, but this time they were not as careful. J.B. tensed as he watched them.

J.B. could see that their rage was driving them forward. Their eyes were no longer sweeping the roadway or the tree line. *'Wait, maintain your discipline. Don't get careless,'* he wanted to yell.

They stopped. J.B. sucked in his breath, *'do they see the trip wires,'* he asked himself, leaning forward to see if the wind had blown the covering snow away from them. The squad leader called to his men, and they turned to look at him. He waved them forward, but they stood still.

J.B. realized they were looking at the Major's driver, slumped in the snow beside the jeep. The advance team could see the body and suspected a trap, the squad leader could not. He just wanted them to go forward, and clear the way for the rest of the squad to advance.

Their rage had dissipated, replaced by revulsion of the carnage before them. *'I bet they've never seen anything like this,'* J.B. thought.

His hunch was proved correct when one of the advance team spewed vomit across the back of the man in front of him. Almost instantly, all three of them were bent forward retching, their weapons dropped into the snow beside the road.

J.B. heard the squad leader vent his rage, as he ran forward with all caution abandoned. The squad followed him.

119

As the leader reached the first man, he grabbed him and shoved him forward, toward the staff car. The soldier stumbled, snagged the trip wire with his boot and detonated the claymores.

J.B. dropped onto his belly, but could not turn his face away from the hell before him.

Each of the four daisy-chained mines spewed out their messengers of death, sweeping through the target zone and shredding the soldiers.

J.B. raised himself to a kneeling position and surveyed the scene. He saw torn bodies, bone, and blood everywhere. The odor of opened bodies rode the wind into the brush, flooding over J.B.

He had seen men killed in battle, but this ambush that he had laid was such a waste of fine men. He was torn between his critical analysis of their carelessness in the final approach, and pride in the efficient manner in which he had laid the ambush.

He was amazed at how quickly the wind was covering their blood with new snow. J.B. knew that more men would come soon, wondering what had happened to their comrades. *'The sight of this will slow them down. The time they will spend in examining this scene will give us an advantage in our run for the sea. But they will put the alert out and come in pursuit of us,'* J.B. said to himself.

J.B. knew the brutality of the ambush would make his enemy all the more determined, and he knew that there would be no mercy if they caught up to him. But then he expected none.

Sighing in acceptance of that which was beyond his control, he kneeled there in the snow at the edge of the forest and prayed.

J.B. did not ask forgiveness for that which he had done. He felt no remorse for the lives he and his Texans had just taken. He did not consider it murder even though he had killed with no consideration of taking captives or of leaving the escort alive.

He was a soldier, killing his enemy under the color of office, and while in uniform. Survivors would have been able to point out their direction of exit and to bear arms in their pursuit. One who leaves an enemy alive on the field and capable of harming him is a fool.

If the circumstances had been reversed, he would not have expected to be treated any differently. He did ask for Divine guidance and vision as his team ran toward their deliverance.

J.B. said his Amen, rose from the snow, adjusted his weapon, and hurried after the team. It was now run to the coast or die in this frozen Siberian forest.

Chapter 13

Cheyenne Mountain

Nikita was immersed in her thoughts. She was staring at her reflection in the shadowed window as the miles rolled away. She became conscious of a voice, a distant hum insistently pushing its' way in, disrupting her thoughts.

"Nikita...Nikita!"

She moved to free her arm from the hand that was grasping it while turning toward the voice. Her hand was roughly pushed away, and there was one more violent shake.

"Nikita snap out of it. Look at me. Focus on me," Special Agent Mayfield urged.

The voice turned from a blurry blot in front of her to the defined face of her captor.

"Let go of me," she said.

Mayfield took his hand away and said, "You've been whimpering and rocking back and forth. It was pretty weird, Nikita. You must have been deep in some rather unpleasant memories."

"Yes, well I'm back now," she said.

"Good, because we are approaching Cheyenne Mountain, and I need you to pay attention to what I'm about to tell you.

This is a military installation, a prison. Once we are inside the facility, you will be stripped and receive a full body search. That means all your body cavities will be searched.

You will be photographed, fingerprinted, and required to shower. You will be issued prison clothing and taken to the medical wing for a physical and dental exam.

You will be assigned a room, but make no mistake about it, you are in prison.

The door will be metal with no handle on the inside. There will be a slot through which your food will be passed to you. You will take all your meals inside your room until we finish processing you into the system.

Your room will have a metal bed frame mounted to the wall and equipped with a mattress, blanket, and pillow. There are a toilet and a sink, but no shower facility. You will not be allowed out of the room for another shower until we finish the in-processing.

You will be under constant video and audio surveillance. Every action and every word will be recorded. Do not have any expectation of privacy because you will not have any.

Once we are ready, we will start our interrogation. It will be an enhanced interrogation, Nikita. We are not going to subject you to torture or deprive you of food, sleep, warmth, etc. But we are going to inject you with drugs that will reduce your desire to resist our efforts. Do you understand what I have told you?"

"Yes, of course, I understand. Do I have a choice in any of this?" Nikita asked.

"None," Mayfield responded.

"I take it no one will know I am here and you will keep me as long as you like, is that right?"

"You are an enemy of the United States caught in the theft of classified information critical to the defense of our Nation. You have killed two of our agents during the act of theft.

You are not an enemy combatant, and are not subject to the provisions of the Geneva Convention nor any other international treaty.

We will squeeze the last drop of intelligence we can out of you, and then you will cease to exist except as a number that has to be fed three times a day.

You have no future, and no hope other than to make your captivity as comfortable as possible by cooperating with us."

Nikita smiled at Mayfield. "That is clear enough. I acknowledge I am caught as you say *red-handed* and will cooperate in hopes that you will keep your word and make my captivity as comfortable as possible. And maybe, after I prove myself, you will grant me a little privacy for the very personal things of life."

"That could be," Mayfield said.

"We're here," the driver called from the front seat.

Nikita looked forward and gasped. She was overwhelmed at her first sight of the place where the rest of her life would be spent.

The Suburban slowed as it approached the mountain. Nikita leaned forward for a better view. She glanced over at Mayfield who smiled at the confused expression on her face. Nikita turned back to look out of the windshield and considered what she was seeing.

The pavement they were driving on seemed to disappear into a shadow on the face of the mountain. As they drew nearer she could see that the road continued into the shadow, which was a cleverly disguised opening, cut into a crease of the granite face of the mountain.

The lights of the Suburban were turned on, and Nikita saw steel doors swing open. Behind those doors was the second set of doors. These consisted of bars with the approach guarded by metal spikes protruding up out of the pavement.

The Suburban stopped, and the driver shifted the transmission into park. He pulled a red placard from under the seat, and hung it onto the rearview mirror. Nikita saw that the placard had the word *Firearms* printed in large white letters across the red background.

Nikita heard a rumbling noise that shook the heavy Suburban in which they sat. She saw the first set of doors sliding closed behind the vehicle and winced at the solid sound of the lock slamming into place.

They were bathed in white lights so bright that it was impossible to see out while everything within the vehicle was brilliantly exposed. *'So much for the privacy tinting,'* Nikita thought.

The hum of a speaker being opened was heard and then a metallic voice saying, "Attention occupants. Remain inside the vehicle, with the

doors closed. Do not move from the position you occupy. We are going to scan your vehicle now."

"What's that about?" Nikita asked.

"Just routine security," the driver responded. "They were expecting us, and know who we are, but out of an abundance of caution, they will check the vehicle for explosive charges, hidden passengers, and of course firearms. That's why I put the placard on the mirror.

We will get a full body scan so they will see the weapons we are carrying as well as those stored in the vehicle. Not to disclose them would result in our being locked in place here until they were satisfied we are legit."

The blinding lights went off, and Nikita could see armed men in uniform surrounding the car. Two of the men were holding what appeared to be disks mounted at the end of long wands. She guessed they passed these along, over and under the vehicle to affect the scan.

The spikes withdrew into the pavement, the bars slid up, and the driver drove forward into the tunnel. A fifteen-minute drive along the well-lighted tunnel brought them to a series of buildings, built side by side, and upward into the mountain.

The driver parked the Suburban. Nikita watched as a team of three men and one woman approached the vehicle. Each was armed and wearing military-style uniforms with badges on their chests.

As they approached the car, the team split with the woman coming to the door of the vehicle behind which Nikita sat. The woman opened the door and said to Nikita, "I am Officer Taliffore of the United States Air Force Security Police. Step from the vehicle and follow my commands."

Nikita stepped out of the vehicle, and faced the officer. "Do you have any firearms or other weapons on your person?" the officer asked.

"No, I am a prisoner," Nikita responded.

"Lift your arms straight out from your sides, at shoulder height, with the palms facing up," the officer instructed.

Nikita did as she was told, and stood still as the officer conducted a quick frisk of her person. "Put your arms down and turn to face the vehicle," was the next instruction.

Nikita did, and then heard, "Place your hands behind your back, with the back of each hand against the back of the other." Nikita complied and felt the cold steel of handcuffs as they were snapped into place.

"Clear," the officer called to her team members.

"Clear," each of the others responded.

The officer stepped away from Nikita and said, "Follow the others as they enter the building."

Nikita saw that other officers had taken the firearms of her captors, but had not handcuffed them. Together they walked through a series of mechanically controlled gates and into the building.

Nikita glanced around at the lobby. Cold grey walls, polished stone floors, and cameras everywhere were her first impression. *'Yep, I'm in until they say I can go'* was her thought.

"We are leaving you in the custody of Officer Tallifore," Mayfield said. She will take you through the first part of the in-processing as I explained earlier. We will be back in a few days to begin our conversation."

"Why are you leaving? Please don't make me wait. I'm ready to get this over with, so I can get settled in. I will tell you everything you want to know now. Just don't leave me hanging here with no showers and no privacy," Nikita said.

"Go with the officer. She will take you to your new home," Mayfield said as he walked away.

Nikita's shoulders slumped as she accepted her fate. She looked at the officer who pointed for her to walk forward, into her life as an enemy of the United States.

Chapter 14

Run To The Sea

J.B. quickly covered the distance between him and the fast-moving team. He whistled as he approached the last man. The man turned, and J.B. could see that an arctic mask covered his face, but he recognized the weapon in his hand to be that of Johnes.

'Good. Sonny has Shooter on the team's six so he can use the scoped rifle on any chasers,' J.B. thought. He nodded to Johnes and ran on to his customary place in the middle of the line. Only then did he allow himself to take notice of the weather.

What he saw caused J.B. to wince. The clouds seemed to be dragging their dark bellies across the tops of the trees as they raced along, driven by the ever-increasing wind.

The snowfall was heavier, and J.B. figured the temperature or least the chill factor had dropped dramatically with the increased wind speed. He was grateful for the protection of the trees but realized it was a double-edged sword because they slowed the team's progress.

The team pushed forward without incident for the next forty-five minutes. Wade turned to face them from his place at the head of the column. He raised his right arm with his mitten flat open and then lowered the arm keeping the glove open to a half rest position. Each member knew that Wade was reducing their pace by half. It was the only rest break they would take as they pushed for the coast.

J.B. took the opportunity to pull his map from the inside of his parka. He located the ambush site, and considered how far their pace had taken them in the last forty-five minutes. He figured they had another seventy-five minutes to their extraction point.

'It's time,' J.B. thought. He pulled the black box from where it was clipped to his parka. He flipped the power button to the on position, and watched as the green light pulsed once, twice, a third time, and then stopped pulsing and remained on.

The transmitter was sending out a signal that the command center on Little Diomede could monitor. *'We're now hot,'* J.B. thought. Not only would his forces on Little Diomede know he was moving and be able to track his progress, but there was always the chance that the Soviet watchers on Big

Diomede would be able to defeat their scramble, and vector in on him also.

The winter storm had now become a blizzard. J.B. knew he could not maintain normal distance in the column because visibility was fast approaching zero. Men lost in a whiteout were dead men.

He moved each man up, so they were putting their foot in the track of the man in front as soon as he picked his foot up. Working his way forward he tightened the whole column.

As he moved up, he took the opportunity to check on Jake's condition. The traitor seemed to be keeping pace. Jake lifted his head as he sensed J.B. staring at him. He nodded at J.B. and pointed forward as if to say, *'don't worry about me keep moving forward."*

His face was covered in the arctic mask J.B. had given him as they moved from the ambush site, but J.B. could see his eyes. He remembered that Jake had said he was a prisoner and was not a willing participant in the Soviet scheme. J.B. had heard what he thought was sincerity in Jake's voice when he said, "I just want to go home."

'I wonder. Is this a kid who screwed up and made it worse by running or is he...,' J.B. was asking himself when the flat crack of a rifle turned him to the rear of the column.

J.B. saw Shooter down on one knee. Pushing out from the front of his parka was a huge red bubble.

Johnes bent forward and lowered his head to look at it. J.B. kneeled in front of him and the bubble burst, spraying Johnes' blood across the front of J.B.'s parka.

Johnes said, "Run," and collapsed on his face in the snow.

The team fanned back to set up a perimeter blocking the trail, and providing cover for J.B. as he lifted Johnes' body onto his shoulder.

J.B. knew that it was a sniper that had taken Johnes. One man, not a squad or they would be pouring fire into the Texans. *'Does he have radio contact with others?'*

J.B. guessed that this was one of many dispatched in different directions with the hope of crossing the team's trail. If so, he would have a radio and would have by now reported contact with the team. *'I bet his orders were to take one of us down, hoping we would go to ground and give them time to close on us. That* means *the chasers are on their way,'* J.B. reasoned.

J.B. moved Johnes body to the shelter of a fallen tree, and then moved back to the team. He scanned the forest behind them but could see nothing. The sniper was hanging back waiting for re-enforcements or for the team to move again so he could take another shot without being seen.

'Think,' J.B. told himself. *'Where would you be if you were the sniper?'*

J.B. surveyed the forest before him. He sectioned it off in his mind, and then examined each section. He saw nothing.

No signs of escaping breath, no movement, nothing. His eyes came back to a giant pine that had fallen during some long past storm. Later storms or just the ravages of time had caused others to fall over and around it.

The thicket created by these rotting giants provided the opportunity for a man to lie on the trunk of the dead tree and still be covered by the brush.

'Pretty slick,' J.B. thought. *'This guy knows his stuff. He is lying there, out of the snow, protected from the wind with an elevated view of the trail. It is a perfect shooting platform.'*

J.B. looked back to check on his team. Each man was focused on him, waiting for his lead. J.B. turned his face toward the sniper's nest, lifted his M-14, clicked the selector to full auto and leveled it on the thicket. He pressed the trigger and swept the barrel back and forth across the site, splintering the brush with a full magazine.

When J.B. started firing so did the others. As one they had risen and advanced as they fired, each man dropping empty magazines and re-loading as they moved.

J.B. raised his right arm with his hand closed into a fist. The advance stopped, and each man ceased firing. J.B. moved up to the fallen tree trunk, where he had judged the sniper to be laying.

He saw the blood first. He leaned over and looked down into the bottom of the brush thicket. The M-14's had done their work. The remains of what once was a man lay in the crimson snow.

J.B. turned and waved the team forward. "Two of you, pull that mess out of there and prop it against that tree right there, next to the trail. I want the chasers to see what we did to him. We need to make them think about being cautious, to slow them down some and this ought to do it."

He looked at Johnes' body and said, "Sonny you take Johnes' rifle. You are now our Shooter. Somebody grab Johnes. He's going home with us. We will take turns carrying him. Reload. I want every man to have a full magazine with one in the chamber. Pick up your empty magazines. Let's move."

J.B. turned and led the team forward. Carrying Johnes slowed their advance. J.B. refused to think of it as a retreat. At the end of an hour, they saw a break in the clouds. J.B. could tell that the storm was passing over and that the extraction chopper would have a window to fly through. *'Fifteen more minutes maybe twenty and we can stop,'* he thought.

He looked back at his team and saw the exhaustion on their faces, in the slump of their shoulders and in how they were dragging their feet through the snow rather than the crisp march they had at the beginning of this run to the sea. *'They are truly on their last legs,'* he thought.

J.B. unclipped the transmitter and looked at it. The green light held steady. That meant it was still sending their position.

He knew that if the signal was being received and if the command had their position, then they knew how close the team was to the sea, and the chopper would already be in the air. They should not be on that beach long before the slick set down.

J.B. ran along the column encouraging each man, "Almost there. Hold on, and we will be eating a hot T-bone steak in Nome tonight. Just hold on."

And on they ran. Then they heard the sea. It seemed a shot of adrenaline had been pumped into each heart. Burning lungs became stronger, trembling legs were steadied and renewed as the Texans reached the tree line. They stood staring out across the beach and over the storm-tossed sea.

J.B. allowed them a few seconds and then pulled them together. "The chopper should be in the air. Still, we need security. Set it up and remain vigilant. We've come too far to let them take us now.

Jake, go to each man and collect his empty magazines. Torres, give him enough loose rounds to reload the mags. Jake, screw with us, and I will open your belly and leave you here with your guts in your hands.

Wade, take Johnes' weapon and watch the beach and the sea. I want every eye on that forest from which we just ran."

J.B. moved to the middle of the arc the team formed. He dropped behind a big Red Oak, and took a quick survey of the field of fire he had in front of him.

He glanced to his right and left and saw the team doing the same thing. He saw Sonny had Jake with him. Jake was lying on his back, sucking air so loud he could be heard over the crashing waves. "Jake, get busy loading those magazines," J.B. ordered.

J.B. turned onto his side and surveyed the beach. The chopper could set down anywhere, but he saw a great place down the beach some forty yards. There was a collection of boulders about head high to a normal sized man. They appeared to have been placed there to form a gun emplacement.

They were covered with ice as the spray from the waves breaking in front of them froze on contact. *'Icy, but still a good fighting position if push comes to shove,'* he thought.

A closer inspection showed him that the boulders fit together so precisely that there was only one way in and one way out of the circle they formed, unless you crawled over them.

'Wow,' he thought, *'we don't want to go in there now because of that spray, but if we must, we can hold up there and make any poor soul coming for us pay a high price. Then we can scoot right out of that little opening and onto the chopper. In the meantime, the chopper can maintain a front forward firing profile or take a half turn and loose those door guns on any target.'*

"We got company, boss," Burtoff called.

J.B. flipped onto his belly as the team opened fire. J.B. saw in front of him a squad-sized force of men. He recognized that these were N.K.V.D. troops, border guards, not regular army.

They were disciplined and well trained. J.B. watched with a practiced eye as the border guards spread into a firing line and went to ground. Their return fire was steady and controlled.

J.B. knew that the longer this battle lasted the less chance he had of getting his team off of the island. He could see the antenna of a field radio sticking up over the log in the exact middle of the enemy's formation.

'*Damn,*' he thought. '*There will be more on the way.*' He looked back to the sea. No boats yet, but he knew they would be coming too. '*Now is the time for us to move to those rocks,*' he said to himself.

He turned to Wade, who had moved up beside him when the fight started. "Lyn, I want you to move from position to position and tell them we are going to make a stand in that collection of rocks there on the left side of the beach. Tell them to watch me.

When I give the signal, I want us to advance to the rear in two-person fire teams. The first group in the rocks will cover everyone else. Got it? Okay, go."

J.B. watched as Wade began his move and wished for a radio. He glanced back at the sea and at the sky above one more time. Both were still empty.

By now the firing had stopped, as each side considered their next move. Jake thought what his opposite number over there was thinking. The N.K.V.D. knew they could wait. That's what he would do if he were in their position. Soon they would have enough troops, boats and even air support to encircle and take the team.

J.B. called to Sonny in the lull, "Sonny, give Jake that grenade launcher and send him over here to me." J.B. watched as Sonny handed the weapon to Jake, saw Jake work the sling of the launcher over his shoulder, roll over and began his crawl through the snow.

J.B. saw no sign of hesitation in Jake. He considered it strange considering his begging back at the ambush site. Jake jumped up and scampered the last few yards to J.B. and, as he did so, the N.K.V.D. opened fire on him.

'*Stupid kid,*' J.B. thought as he watched a round pluck at the hem of Jake's parka.

"That was close," Jake said as he dropped to the ground beside J.B.

J.B. took some time to consider Jake. What he saw were eyes clear of fear, an open and smiling countenance and a readiness to obey.

"Jake, we are in a hell of a mess. The odds are against us getting out of this. My question is this, if they take us will you go back over to them or will you refuse to help them and stand with us?" J.B. asked.

"Hey Sergeant, I messed up big time. I know that. I also know that I am

132

going to do some hard time behind this, but I hope you believe me when I say that I would rather do hard time in an American prison than live free in their society. I'm asking you to let me fight. Let me become an American soldier again, please sergeant."

J.B. thought for a minute and decided to trust his gut. "Okay, but if you cross us, I will personally bust a cap on you. Do you believe me?"

Jake nodded, and J.B. said, "I'm going to move up and take cover behind that stump off to the right. I want you to skinny over there to where Torres is laying and get that bag of grenades he has. Then I want you to join me there at the stump.

I am going to cover you as you get on one knee behind that pine next to the stump, and lob those grenades to cover the team as they run for those rocks."

Jake slithered through the snow to Torres. He reached for the bag of grenades, and Torres slammed the butt of his rifle down on his hand.

Jake screamed out in pain.

J.B. watched as Jake talked with Torres and then pointed towards his sergeant. Torres followed Jakes point and saw J.B. nod his head.

He released his hold on the bag and shoved Jake away from him. J.B. moved to the stump and Jake slid in behind the pine. J.B. asked, "How bad is that hand hurt?"

"It hurts but it is not broken, and I can still operate this launcher. I did really well when training with this weapon at Fort Bliss," Jake said.

J.B. got the attention of the team and waved them out toward the rocks. As the first team moved out, J.B. said, "Now Jake, let's see just how good you are with those grenades."

Jake smiled at J.B. and rose to one knee, leaned around the tree and fired the first grenade. He aimed it for the antenna sticking up in the middle of the enemy formation.

J.B. watched as the fragmentation grenade arced up and descended over the antenna. It exploded before it hit the ground.

'Perfect. Not only is the radio now out of action but hopefully, the leader of

133

the opposition was next to it and is dead ,' J.B. thought.

Jake continued to wreak havoc with the grenades even as the N.K.V.D. poured fire onto the stump and pine sheltering Jake and his sergeant. J.B. could see that the last two of the team were moving back to the rocks. He kept watching as they entered the cover of the boulders and started laying down covering fire for him and Jake.

J.B. tapped Jake on the shoulder and mouthed, "One more and let's boogie."

Jake nodded with understanding. He dropped the grenade launcher and smiled at J.B. He then reached into the bag and pulled the last two grenades out. He flipped one to J.B. and kept the other. Together they pulled the pins and heaved the grenades into the N.K.V.D. position.

They were up and running for the rocks before the grenades exploded. As they left their cover, the border guards stood to fire at them, and the grenades detonated in their midst, dropping the exposed troops.

J.B. and Jake slid behind the rocks, and Jake laughed. *'Strange,'* he thought, *'but this is so exhilarating. Damned if I'm not a combat veteran.'*

He laughed again and pushed all thought of the prison cell awaiting him out of his mind. *'If I have a limited time to live free, this is the way to do it. Right here, with these warriors. And warriors they are,'* he thought as his eyes wandered back and forth over the embattled troops. *Man, I wish I had a flag to hoist. How I would love to see, the stars and stripes flying right here, over our stone fort, on the beach of the Russian Bear,'* grinned.

J.B turned to scan the sea and saw three specks on the far horizon racing in toward them. He realized the pilots had a fix on their signal and were riding the beam, with their course centered on the stone fort.

"Burtoff," J.B. yelled. "See those freedom birds, there on the horizon? They have us located, but they don't know that we are engaged. We need to pop smoke to let them know this LZ is hot. Do you have any red smoke?"

"No, but I have plenty of orange. They will get it once they see it is not the normal white smoke we pop for extraction," Burtoff replied.

"That will work. Wait until they are halfway in, and then pop that orange smoke," J.B. said.

J.B. turned back to the forest and gasped. The tree line was now filled with the olive-green uniforms of the Soviet army.

'*Those are combat troops. Their commander will not hesitate to order them to charge across the open beach to overwhelm us. But, they will have to run through our fire for forty yards with no cover. We have a chance to stop them, but we will need every round we have,*' J.B. reasoned. "Hold your fire. Stay low, don't give them a target. They only way they can reach us is by charging across the beach. If they come, we will need every round. Wait for my order to fire," J.B. told his Texans.

J.B. turned back and watched as a Soviet Captain, stepped from the tree line in a show of contempt for the Texans. The Captain glanced once toward the rocks and then lifted his glasses and focused on the helicopters. J.B. saw him smile as he lowered the glasses and stepped back inside the tree line and pointed toward the choppers.

'He's going to wait. Either he has air support on the way, or He thinks he can take the choppers and us. He better hope that air support gets here or the choppers' rockets and machine guns will chew him and his command up,' J.B. thought.

"Pop that smoke, Burtoff," J.B. called.

"It's a little early, boss," Burtoff responded.

"No, I want them to see it now and know this beach is hot. Maybe too hot, but let's give them plenty of notice," J.B. said.

Burtoff crawled to the edge of the stones and rolled the smoke canister out, onto the beach. The orange smoke spewed up, and the wind carried it away, straight toward the Soviets waiting in ambush inside the tree line.

"That's it. Throw another, throw them all toward the trees. The pilots will see the concentration of smoke, and will understand the enemy is there," J.B. shouted.

Burtoff handed one canister to Jake and took the last one for himself. "Let's do this right," he said to Jake.

Burtoff ran from the stone shelter to a shallow cleft in the beach. Jake followed him. They heaved the smoke canister directly toward where the Captain had stood. Their aim was dead on. Smoke spewed out and the wind wrapped it like a cloak around the Soviet troops.

Burtoff and Jake ran back to cover as the first two Choppers swept in over the beach. The whoosh of seventy-millimeter rockets filled the air as the pilots unloaded on the smoke.

Rocket after rocket found its' mark. J.B. and his Texans watched as trees, sand, and flesh mixed in a vortex of high explosives. The Slicks swung broadside, and the machineguns erased all life inside the tree-line.

'How in the hell did that commander think he could take those choppers? Or, did his Russian bosses want to track them across and strike them on the U.S.

side of the line,' J.B. wondered.

The third and final chopper set down just outside the stone fort, and the Texans ran for its' open doors. They handed Johnes' body up first, and then they scrambled in. The team was still settling in as the pilot lifted off and swung out over the sea.

The crew chief was reaching for the door when J.B. put his hand on it. He leaned out and looked back at the beach. The first two gunships had now disengaged and were already out over the Strait, and closing on them quickly. Nothing moved on the beach. J.B. could smell the burning flesh.

He knew it would take a while for the scene from that frozen beach to leave his dreams.

He pulled the transmitter from his parka and tossed it out of the door and into the sea, *'just in case the Soviets did have a fix on it,'* he thought.

Then he leaned back and nodded at the chief. The chief slammed the door, as spray splashed inside the cabin.

The pilots dropped the birds to the wave top and raced for home. Two and one-half miles and they would be over American water. A blink of the eye at the one-hundred and thirty-five miles an hour these slicks were hitting.

J.B. looked at his team. No one was talking; each was locked in his thoughts. And then there was the dead face of Johnes.

J.B. turned his head toward Jake. Jake was staring at Johnes and lifted his eyes when he felt J.B. staring at him. "Would have been better if it had been me," Jake said.

"Damned straight it would have," Torres grunted.

The team shifted, but no one else said anything.

"Mr. Perkins, pick up the headset please," the cabin speaker squawked.

J.B. stood and lurched forward, grabbed the headset, and swung the mike down over his mouth, "Perkins," he said.

"This is the pilot. We are in the clear, there is no pursuit, and there is nothing showing on radar. We are now crossing the midpoint and will be feet dry in about one-hundred and twenty seconds. Sit back and relax, because we have orders to take you inland and set you down.

Once we clear the Strait, my orders are to throttle back to eighty miles an hour, to conserve fuel. Sorry, but you boys are not going to Nome. Give me ninety minutes, and I will land you on friendly soil."

"Roger that." J.B. hung the headset back on the rack and sat down.

He wondered where they were headed, but knew the pilot wouldn't tell him over a clear channel, and besides it didn't matter. As long as it was friendly soil, he would be stepping out onto. He breathed a sigh of relief and thought, *'sure wish it was Texas soil.'*

"Okay, guys. We are in the clear. It's over, so relax as much as you can. We're ninety minutes to touch down.

Eject your magazines, open the breach, and be sure your weapons are safe. Leave your pistols holstered until we step down from the aircraft," J.B. said to the team.

He knew they were coming off the adrenaline rush of the extraction. That combined with the fatigue of their run to the sea and it was amazing that they were still functioning. J.B. checked again on Jake and saw that he was out cold.

'These warriors will rebound quickly. In a couple of days, they will be back working the gate, on town patrol, or chasing AWOL's. But what about Jake? Those wanting to question him will have to wait. He will need time to recover. Time is one thing Jake is going to have plenty of,' J.B. thought as he closed his eyes.

Chapter 15

The Process

Nikita stood under the warm water and allowed it to run freely over every muscle, and into every crevice of her violated body.

Hot tears gushed from her eyes and flowed down her face, mixing with the pounding stream from the shower. Gradually she gained control of her emotions and began to relax. As she did, she could feel her taut muscles loosen, the tears stopped, and she lifted her head and turned it to the left where Officer Tallifore stood watching her.

Nikita dropped her head but did not attempt to shield her body from the officer's view. She was broken, besides there was nothing Tallifore and the others had not seen.

The process had been all Special Agent Mayfield had promised, and then some. After stripping her naked, they had examined every inch of her physical being. They had probed, pulling and stretching with their latex covered fingers.

Her weeping, brought on by such degradation, caused the examiner to stop and order another sedative be administered.

They had given her a brief respite to recover and then came the x-rays, sonograms and radiation scans. Every tooth, every filling, even her nails were inspected for any method of communication, transmission, recording, or hidden information. Then officer Tallifore led her into a room where a woman cut her hair off and shaved her head, under her arms and her pubic areas.

"Why?" Nikita had cried to Tallifore.

Tallifore had just lifted an eyebrow and told the woman to continue. When she was fully shaved, Tallifore led her into a room where she stood while women with their faces covered by masks and respirators sprayed her with a yellowish tan liquid. They made her bend forward and pull her buttocks apart and sprayed the fluid between her opened cheeks.

Then it was finally over. The women pulled a metal stool into the room and told her to sit on it while the spray dried. One leaned forward and whispered, "Please forgive us. We know how humiliating all this is. Just try to relax, and things will get better."

Nikita sat on the stool and wept. *'How did I fall so far? From a woman serving her nation with pride and honor to a breathing hunk of flesh to be pushed, probed, and sprayed like some animal.'*

Tallifore appeared in the door and called her down the hall and into the shower. She lifted a bar of soap from the dish above the shower control. It was still wrapped in paper, and she was comforted to know that no one else had used it.

She ran the bar over her body, working up a rich lather. She re-visited each area probed, shaved and sprayed, coating them with the cleansing suds.

She was twice through the routine when Tallifore called out, "That's enough. Finish up and step out."

Nikita turned once more under the rinsing spray and shut the shower off. She stepped over the lip of the shower pan and out onto the floor and stood before Tallifore.

The officer pointed to an X painted on the floor. Nikita stepped on it, and Tallifore pressed a button on the wall. Warm air flooded from the vents just above her and Nikita luxuriated under its soothing caress.

Tallifore allowed her a few minutes and then pressed the button again, and the air stopped flowing. Tallifore then pointed to a pale blue dress folded on a shelf mounted to the wall. Laying on top of the dress were a plain white bra, a pair of white cotton panties and a pair of slip-on cloth shoes.

"Dress," Tallifore said.

Nikita dressed and was led down yet another hallway with cameras, swiveling to watch her every step. Tallifore called out, "Stop."

Nikita stopped and stood still facing away from the officer. She heard Tallifore insert a key into a lock, turn the key and swing the door open.

"Face right," Tallifore said.

Nikita turned to face the wall. She could see Tallifore out of the corner of her eye as the officer checked to ensure there was no one in the room.

"Face left and enter the room, Tallifore ordered.

Nikita did as she was told and found herself walking into what she recognized as an interrogation room. There was a table with four chairs in the center of the room. Sitting in the corner of the room was a second table equipped with leather wrist and ankle restraints. *'They won't need that,'* Nikita thought to herself.

"Sit at the center table facing away from the door," Tallifore said.

Nikita sat and then turned to face Tallifore. "Do not look at me," Tallifore said.

Nikita turned away and said, "Can we talk?"

"We have nothing to talk about," Tallifore responded in her clipped military manner.

Nikita knew it was useless to push her, so she sat with her hands folded in her lap and waited. It was not long until she heard a key being inserted into the lock. Instinctively she turned toward the door.

"Face forward," Tallifore barked.

Nikita turned back and felt the sweep of wind as the door was pushed open. She listened as footsteps approached the table. She looked up, into the face of Special Agent Mayfield and then Special Agent Box. Despite herself, she found a smile gathering on her face.

Her eyes must have given her feelings away as Mayfield said softly, "Hello, Nikita. I know you've been through a lot today, but there have been some developments that require us to move the interview schedule up. Time is critical to us, and we must start gathering information from you. Are you going to cooperate?"

Nikita nodded her head vigorously and said, "Yes. I will answer every question, and I will not lie. I will do whatever I can to improve my circumstances. Please let me help myself. I don't want to be treated like an animal. Please ask your questions."

"I must tell you that while we do want and value your cooperation, you are still an enemy of the state, responsible not only for the loss of critical defense secrets, but the death of two fine soldiers.

Your living conditions might improve, but Nikita you need to understand that you are going to be in prison for the rest of your life. As a prisoner you

141

will be subjected to necessary security provisions."

"I know. But to have some privacy. Please, just let me have some dignity," Nikita whimpered.

"We'll see, but first let's get to this. Nikita, do you admit that you are an agent of the Soviet Union, trained in espionage?" Mayfield asked.

"Yes, I do," Nikita responded.

"Were you assigned to operate in Fairbanks?" Mayfield asked.

"Yes," Nikita nodded.

"Was Fairbanks your first assignment in the U.S.?" the agent asked.

"No. My first assignment was in Maryland." Nikita said.

"What did you do there?" he asked.

"I was to get close to the soldiers from Fort Meade and gather information about the Nike Hercules units assigned to the East Coast Protection District and N.S.A. headquarters," she responded.

"Hey boss, this is interesting but we better get to the questions about Jake," Box said.

Mayfield scowled and turned to face Box. Finally, he said, "Don't interrupt me again." Box shrugged, but sat silent.

"Why do you American intelligence agents shrug so much? We were taught that such habits mark you. It is true, don't you think?" Nikita said.

Mayfield asked, "How did you come to meet Jake?"

"I was planted in the Polaris, because we knew that G.I.s were going there for the American girls. Jake was always there. We spotted him as a source because of his lack of social skills and shy demeanor.

So, I just sat and waited. Finally, he approached me, and it was all downhill from there.

I played the girl-next-door, abandoned by a wayward husband, who had to become a working girl to survive. Jake didn't buy it. I could tell he had his

142

doubts.

We thought about moving on to another, but by then Demetrio knew he was in the five-sixty-second ADA. We were most interested in the missile defenses, and I was told to do what I needed to keep him on the hook.

I doubted he was ever going to get up the nerve to ask me for sex, so I took the initiative and led him upstairs. It only took one time and then how do you Americans say it, *the hook was set.*

He was putty in my hands, and I felt sure he would give me anything I wanted. But Demetrio, and the others, wanted an insurance policy, so to speak.

That is why Demetrio recorded our sexual activities and copied his identification. We were going to confront him and threaten to expose him if he did not give us the information we wanted. But it didn't come to that," Nikita explained.

"Wait, wait. You said a couple of things I want to clarify. You said that you were most interested in the missile defenses and then you said that there were others besides Demetrio? Is that right, did you say that others were directing you besides Demetrio?" Mayfield asked.

Nikita nodded her head, "Yes, but I do not know who the others were.

I knew they were in Fairbanks, and I knew they were watching me. But I also knew they would never let me know who they were. That is part of the training. You are told that you will be given only the information you need to operate. That is a safeguard against this sort of circumstance. If I knew who or where they were, I would be giving them up to you at this very instant."

Mayfield hesitated a minute, and then asked, "How did you come to know Demetrio?"

"He met me at the airport when I came over from Maryland," she responded.

"He was your handler then?" Box asked.

"No, he was my contact with the managers. He saw to it that I had everything I needed, he provided me with instructions, and he made sure I followed them.

He was nice to me, but he represented the managers and saw to it that I obeyed. In short, I was on a chain, and he held the other end," Nikita answered.

"Why were you interested in the missile defense? Did Demetrio tell you that was where their interest lay or did you figure that out for yourself?" Box asked.

Mayfield sighed, and sat back in his chair. Nikita looked from Mayfield to Box, and then back to Mayfield. She arched her eyebrow in question, and Mayfield nodded his head. Then she turned to Box and said, "Both. See, when I got settled in at the Polaris..."

"Wait," Mayfield interrupted. "How did you come to be at the Polaris?"

"I went straight there from the airport. I always suspected that we had someone running or at least helping run the Polaris. Why? Because I moved right in with no questions asked, and no one ever said a word to me about my being so selective about who I accepted as a client."

Then she turned back to Box and said, "Once at the Polaris, it didn't take long for one of the soldiers I took upstairs to answer my questions about his assignment.

When he said he was in the Air Defense Artillery, I knew there was Nike Hercules nearby. And since that had been my focus in Maryland, I put two and two together and came up with four."

"Do you have any idea why your bosses were so interested in the Nike Hercules?" Box asked.

"Sure," Nikita answered. "Because the two points they consider the most advantageous for the invasion of the U.S. mainland, Florida from Cuba, and Alaska across the Bearing Strait, both are protected by Nike Hercules sites.

We know the missiles can be armed with nuclear or conventional warheads, and we know that they could be used as air defense artillery or as cannons against our ground troops.

But we also know that our technology forces have been somewhat successful in breaking through the security firewall to arm and launch the missiles.

What we need is their arming and firing procedures. Then we could arm the warhead and launch the missile against major targets within the U.S., behind the shield.

So, you see, we were trying to use your weapons against those cities that we could not reach from the other side. It was a beautiful plan, was it not?"

"Nikita, does the phrase, *'flying Wolfman Jack'* mean anything to you?" Mayfield asked.

Nikita smiled. "Ah yes, for sure. That is the password for Specialist Five Anthony Weir, who is an internal fire control operator for the Nikes located at Fort Meade.

He boasted to me of his IT savvy and was so proud of his password that he shared it with me. We used that password to get past the firewall and launch one of the birds.

Your army's official explanation was that it was an accidental launch caused by carelessness on the part of the internal fire control van crew. Believe me, it was no accident.

We used that same method to get into the arming and launching sequence for a unit on Okinawa. We broke into their firing progression and launched the missile while the crew was in the pit, running the continuity tests.

Unfortunately, the blast incinerated two and seriously injured another.

This time the official explanation was that a frayed cord lying in a puddle of water shorted out and launched the bird. Did anyone expect that to be believable? An electrical short launches a nuclear weapon?"

"What about the ones in Inchon, Korea, and outside of Miami Florida?" Mayfield asked.

"I heard about them, but I don't know anything about how those launches were accomplished. However, it would follow that our agents were able to penetrate the security systems.

By the way, I never operated in Florida, Korea, or on Okinawa. I say this to point out to you that we have agents everywhere in the U.S.

Your borders are so porous, but it is also so easy to defeat your immigration people. We walk in, and you smile and say welcome to America.

Why is that? Why does a great nation like America invite destruction?" Nikita asked.

Box and Mayfield glanced at each other, then Mayfield looked up at the camera mounted over the door behind Nikita and said, "This seems like a good time for you to join us."

Nikita heard the door open but continued to face forward looking down at the table. She counted the steps and lifted her head just as the new interrogator sat down.

"Hello, Nikita. I am Sam Sorrensby, and I am with the National Security Agency. I have a few questions also. Is that okay with you?"

Nikita thought, 'What if it's not? Are you going to open the gates and let me go with an apology for all the inconvenience?'

She smiled at the man and said, "Sure. As you Americans say, the more, the merrier. Or as one of my favorite clients at the Polaris was prone to say, shoot Luke or give up the gun."

The men laughed, and Sorrensby said, "Back to Jake. A little earlier you said that you had planned on working him and if that didn't produce information, you would have blackmailed him, but then you said it never came to that. What did you mean by that?"

"I mean that Jake was a fool. He was so hot to get back to me that he brought an SOP Manual for the Nike Hercules. When Demetrio saw it, he knew we had all we needed," Nikita smiled.

"So, you are telling me that you did not ask him to bring the manual or to give you information that it contained?" Sorrensby said.

"That's right. Jake messed up, and we were there to take advantage," she responded.

"Did Jake ever give you classified information?" Sorrensby asked.

"No. But I know he would have. It is like I said, he messed up and so we never had to extract the information. By the way, what happened to Jake? Do you have him?" she asked.

"What do you mean? Don't you know where he is?" Sorrensby asked.

146

"No, I don't. I shot the agent named Archie and Jake charged across the room and knocked me over. He picked up a lamp and smashed it into Demetrio's face. He killed Demetrio, it just took a while for him to die.

Jake handcuffed me to Demetrio, flushed the key, gathered up the SOP Manual, and walked out. I haven't seen him since. Where is he?" Nikita asked.

"He defected. Went over to your side, and carried the manual with him. We know the information is already copied and compromised.

We will change everything, but what concerns us is that Jake will continue to use what he knows to counter our changes. Give me your thoughts.

Will the Soviets keep him indefinitely and if so, where? Or do you think they will milk him for what he knows now and then dispose of him?" Sorrensby asked.

Nikita thought a minute. "No, they won't dispose of him as long as you have the Nike Hercules deployed. He knows the procedure and they will keep him to counter your changes. But when he is no longer of any value, and they will either offer him for exchange or kill him."

"That's what we thought," Sorrensby added.

"Let me guess. You are going to send someone to hit him, to stop the flow of information. Is that your plan?" Nikita asked.

"What would you do?" Mayfield asked.

"Kill him. The quicker, the better," Nikita said with a smile.

"Killing doesn't seem to bother you," Box said.

Nikita saw the trap before her. She looked at Box and then shifted her gaze to Mayfield and said, "If I say no that killing does not bother me, then I become a cold-hearted spy who killed your agents without remorse, and that's a strike against the possibility of my conditions in captivity being improved.

On the other hand, if I say why yes, I think killing is horrible, then the question is, then why did you kill our two agents?

You see that I am not bothered by the fact that I killed those two men, so I

147

become a liar, and you don't believe what I say. Strike one, two, three, and that's the old ball game. Lock her up in the darkest, dankest dungeon and throw the key away, right? So, here's my answer. No, killing does not bother me.

Next question, have you killed before? Yes, I have. But not in America. You will think this horrible but all KGB agents must kill before their training is complete."

"We already knew that. But tell us, why did you kill Dikes and Norwood? You had the drop on them. Why not just take their guns, handcuff them, and leave with the SOP?" Box asked.

"That was not an option. I was handcuffed already when I shot the first one, the one you call Dikes. I feared he would be able to overpower me, take my pistol and there was no time.

I knew the second one, Norwood, would be back quickly and I had to be in control by that time. It was unfortunate but necessary," Nikita said.

Sorrensby nodded and pushed back from the table. He turned to Mayfield and said, "We have all we need for now. We want to keep her on ice for future events. She has great insight."

Mayfield stood and extended his hand. Sorrensby stood, shook Mayfield's hand and turned to leave the room. At the door, he turned back and said, "Just for the record, we don't object to giving her some perks. She has done us some good here today."

"Sounds good to us too," Mayfield said.

Sorrensby walked out, and Mayfield turned to Box, "Got anything else, David?"

Box shook his head and stood. "No, not at the moment, boss. I think it was a good session, but that's it for now."

Mayfield turned to Tallifore and said, "Can we put her in a room with a private bath?"

Tallifore responded, "You're the boss. I will walk her to the front gate if you say so."

"No, I don't think we will do that. But do give her a comfortable room with private bath and if you don't mind, be sure she gets a good mattress, some blankets, and one more thing, let's feed her well tonight?" Mayfield said.

"Sure thing. Do you want me to give her a bottle of wine too?" Tallifore said.

The sharpness of the officer's tone caused Mayfield to wince. "Look..."

"No, sir. No look to it. You call the shots. Everything you ask for, she gets," Tallifore said.

"But?" Mayfield left the question lay on the stillness.

"But we have two dead agents. I bet they would like to be in a warm cell with a comfy bed and a hot beefsteak on the table. Who am I to question the FBI and how they handle an enemy of our nation, Sir?" Tallifore spat out.

Mayfield felt the sting, but said nothing.

"Stand up Nikita," Tallifore said.

Nikita stood under the withering glare of the uniformed officer.

"Go out that door and turn right. Down the hall, until I say stop. Move," Tallifore ordered.

Nikita marched out. Tallifore halted her a few feet down the hall, opened the door to a room and told her to step in.

Nikita did, and the door closed behind her. She did not move until the key had turned in the lock. She then relaxed and looked around.

Her cell was a cinder block room with a wood framed cot pushed against one wall; mattress, sheets, blankets, and pillows lay rolled on the cot. At the end of the room was what appeared to be a closet. Nikita walked over to peer inside. It was not a closet but her bathroom, complete with sink, commode, and shower stall.

She paced the length of the room and found it to be exactly fourteen feet long. She stepped off the width and found it to be ten feet wide. There were no windows. No chairs. That was it, there was nothing else.

Nikita rolled out the mattress, spread the sheets and blanket, and stretched out on her bed. Her head was spinning with the day's events as she spiraled down into the darkness and exhaustion sucked her in.

'Good thing I have Mayfield, Box, and Sorrensby in my corner. I have to stay on their good side. Can't let them walk away and leave me with Tallifore,' was her last conscious thought.

Sorrensby was standing in the lobby as Box and Mayfield exited the secure area. He looked up and waved them over.

"I been thinking. If we can get Jake back, what if we were to bring him here and put those two in the same room together?" he asked.

"What, you mean, have them living together?" Mayfield asked.

"No, no. I am not sharing the same cell. I mean if we bring them into the same interrogation session together. You know, set them across from each other at the same table and fire away. That might make for an interesting session. I bet we could use what each said to gain a whole new perspective on this. It might help us in the future," Sorrensby offered.

"You mean you think we might learn something new for our counterintelligence efforts in the future?" Box asked.

"That is what I think. What if we made a team out of these two? I mean we might even set our operation up in the Polaris or the next place like it.

We could learn who was working the troops, and hey we could work them ourselves. Get the weak links out of the chain so to speak. And, I bet there is a lot more in this deal than what we are seeing. Those two get to bouncing things off of each other, and who knows what might pop out," Sorrensby said.

"I like the idea," Mayfield said. "But, we don't have Jake, and unless you know something we don't, there is not much chance of our getting him back."

Sorrensby shifted his gaze away and stared out the front glass a few seconds too long before answering, "Well, I tell you what. No, on second thought, let's leave it there, and I will get back to you in a couple of days." With that, he turned and walked out the door.

Mayfield and Box looked at each other. "That's what one would call a pregnant pause," Box said.

Mayfield rolled his eyes up toward the ceiling and then glanced at Box as if to remind him of the listening devices. Box nodded, and they walked out.

Once outside, Mayfield turned to Box and said, "Sorrensby does know something. I bet there is an operation already launched and given what Sorrensby said it must be one where the first effort is to bring him in and the second is to kill him if the first is not possible."

"I agree. Let's hope they get him back. I would love to sit him down with Nikita," Box said. The agents turned and hustled across the darkening yard toward the bright lights of the cafeteria.

Chapter 16

Friendly Soil

The big Huey slowed, and started its' descent. The crew chief stood up and said, "It won't be but a couple of minutes gents. Gather your stuff and be prepared to exit the aircraft as soon as I open the doors.

I don't know where we are so don't ask me. All I can tell you is that you will be on friendly soil.

There will be a covered deuce and half waiting. Go straight to it and climb in. I need two of you to carry your KIA with you. Sorry, but he goes into the back of the truck. These troops all know enough not to ask questions, but we can't afford to let them see this dead warrior."

"I got him," Torres said.

"Me too," Wade chimed in.

J.B. nodded his agreement and then said, "Be sure you take all your gear. Don't leave anything that can be traced."

The Chopper settled down, and the chief racked the door back. The team jumped from the bird and hurried to the waiting truck. They climbed into the welcoming warmth provided by the gasoline heater. Torres and Wade handed Johnes' body up, and jumped in.

The driver of the truck grabbed the tarp and tucked it inside. "Zip this up guys, and that cooler sitting in the middle there is filled with Colorado Kool-Aid. Go for it."

J.B. made Jake next to him at the far end of the truck. The team was digging for the beer. A few of those on their empty stomachs and their grief at the loss of Johnes might boil over.

"Go easy on that beer," J.B. ordered. "No more than two each. And let me get this over with now. We have been through hell to get Jake back here. We lost Johnes along the way. Nobody regrets that more than me.

But my orders are to deliver this man to the spooks, and that is what I aim to do. Follow?"

The team turned sullen faces toward J.B., but he could see that each man understood the need to hand Jake over to the intelligence guys. They would be okay.

"Want one of these, boss?" Torres held up one of the Coors.

"Not till I hand Jakes over," J.B. answered.

Torres smiled, nodded, and leaned back with his second cold one.

J.B. lifted the tail flap and looked out. They were in a heavily forested area, but J.B. noticed that while not on pavement, the truck was rolling along without much bouncing. Looking down he could see that the route they were taking had been graded. As they pushed along, J.B. began to see troops. *'This must be a base camp,'* he thought.

J.B. dropped the flap and sat back thinking, *'We came back over the Strait, flying in an easterly direction. Just after we went feet dry, the pilot made a turn to the left. We were then flying in a North by East direction.*

We cruised for ninety minutes at eighty miles per hour, so we traveled inland about a hundred and twenty miles. That puts us in the center of the Bering Land Bridge National Preserve. The only base camp in this area is Redstone, a joint operation between the Canadian Four-Fifty-Second Mountain, the U.S. One-Seventy-First Infantry, and the Eight Hundred and Eighth combat engineers out of Wainwright. This place is a launching pad for special ops across the Strait, and to stage resources for use against an invasion by the Soviets. It is a high-security area with a complete blackout on public awareness."

The truck slowed and then stopped. J.B. heard steps approaching the back of the truck. He turned to the team and saw that every eye was watching the canvas flap.

The tailgate dropped, big hands reached up and pushed the flap out of the way, and a booming voice greeted them with, "Offload one at a time. I don't want to see a weapon in any man's hand."

J.B. stood and walked down the steps that had been set up at the back of the truck. The first face he saw was that of Sam Groves.

J.B. noticed that his silver bars of a First Lieutenant had been replaced with the railroad tracks of a Captain. J.B. smiled and saluted. "Good to see

153

you, sir. Congratulations on the promotion."

Groves returned the salute and said, "There are some more promotions coming for our group. But for now, welcome home.

You all have done a hell of a thing in getting that flow of information shut off. The pilot told us that you have a KIA. Who is it?"

"It is Johnes, Sir. We brought him home, as you promised him."

"Good." The Captain turned to a sergeant standing by the foot of the truck.

"Sergeant, I want that man's body handled with all the respect due him. I know you will see to that. Take him to the casualty tent and place a guard on it. Nobody goes in without my express permission. Understood?"

The sergeant spoke to J.B., "I promise you he will be treated right." Then he turned to Groves and said, "Yes, sir. I got it."

The team stood silently while the sergeant sent four men up the ladder to collect Johnes. They handed him down to four more that stood ready to receive him on the ground. They carried him to a waiting pickup, slid his bagged body into the bed, and climbed up to sit on the side rails as the truck eased away with its precious cargo.

"I know you're tired, but get your Texans together and meet me in that twelve man tent just across the way in ten minutes. We debrief, and then you can chow down. I smell beer on the men. I regret that. No more until we get this sorted out," the Captain said.

"What about him?" J.B. nodded at Jake who was standing on his left.

"He goes with these two walking up now," Groves said.

J.B. looked to where the Captain pointed and saw two men in civilian clothing approaching. They stopped in front of the Captain, and the taller one said, "Which one?"

"Me," Jake said.

"Walk in front of me in that direction, and keep walking until I say stop," the tall one said.

Jake turned to J.B. and said, "If I could change any of this, if I could trade

154

places with Johnes I would."

He stuck out his hand and said, "You probably don't want to shake my hand, but I would be honored to shake yours."

J.B. looked at the hand and then reached out and shook it. "You screwed up, Jake. That cost lives. Whatever is next, my advice is this. You can't undo that which is done. But you can do what's right from this point forward. I hope you do."

Jake nodded, then turned and walked away.

J.B. faced the team and said, "Move to the twelve-man tent and wait for the Captain and me."

The team turned and moved to the tent. J.B. watched and could see their fatigue in the way they trudged along. "What happens to him now?" he asked the Captain.

"Who are you referring to sergeant?" the Captain asked.

J.B. smiled, "You mean he no longer exists?"

"Who are we talking about Sergeant?" Groves asked.

Groves clapped J.B. on the shoulder, and they walked toward the tent. The Texans stood as Groves entered, "As you were," he said.

The team settled down on the benches, and Groves began by saying, "You brought our target home alive, and I want to say to you that I know the discipline, focus, and purpose that required. Did you get the SOP Manual?"

"Yes Sir, here it is," Torres stood and handed it to Groves. "And sir, we also got these."

He handed Groves the envelope he had stuffed inside his parka as the other team members stood and gave him the ones they had carried out.

"Great, did you take anything personal off of the bodies?" he asked.

"Yes, sir. We collected their wallets, dog tags, and shoulder patches," J.B. said as he handed them over to Groves.

"Good. The Spooks will love this," the Captain said.

"Now, tell me how it went down. Sergeant, you go first. I want to hear every detail," Groves said as he pulled an empty bench up to face the team.

J.B. carried him through the entire operation. From the time they hit the cold landing zone through the run to the ambush site, the setting of the ambush and then the long wait for the target to appear. He talked about the Soviet Major surveying the bridge and then moving forward, into the ambush.

The breathing was slow and measured as the team relived the operation. They leaned into the memory of the ambush, the killing.

J.B. told about watching the search squad walk into the kill zone and how the claymores had shredded them. As he spoke the sights and smells of the action returned.

He hesitated remembering the bodies dancing in death, as the steel balls raced through them. The odor of the burning flesh, the opened guts and the bits of hair and bone ricocheting off the trees under which he crouched. The squad, hearing it for the first time sat with eyes fixed on J.B.

He told the Captain about the sniper taking Johnes and about how they had left him sitting on the trail for his comrades to see.

The fight at the beach was quick and simple to tell, but J.B. drew it out some taking time to stress the role Jake had played. The team shuffled a little as his report on Tolbert's behavior became more and more favorable.

Finished with his tale, J.B. looked at his Texans and said, "Anyone has anything to add, or if you saw any of it differently, tell the Captain."

Wade responded, "You told it right, boss."

J.B. nodded and turned to the Captain, "That's it."

Groves stood, and the team stood with him. "You leave here at five tomorrow morning. You will go back to Wainwright, and then to Ft. Lewis. You all are so near your release from active duty that it has been decided that you will remain there working with the Armed Forces Police Detachment out of SeaTac until your ETS.

If anybody tries to question or to talk to you about this, let your sergeant know. You can chow down, shower, and grab a couple of hours sleep before

156

liftoff tomorrow morning."

He looked from man to man. Slowly he came to attention and saluted them. They snapped to and returned the salute. Groves walked to the flap of the tent and turned back. "Thank you for your service and may *God bless Texas,*" he said and was gone.

"It's over, so let's wind down. The Captain has arranged for us to have a new set skivvies, socks, fatigues, and boots waiting for us in the shower shack. Let's get squared away, chow down, and get some rest. We lift off at zero five-hundred, so we need to be on station at zero-four-forty-five," J.B. said.

He led the Texans out of the tent, and the tension began to fall away.

Chapter 17

The Proposition

Jake was escorted to a squad tent with nothing but one table and three chairs inside. His escort led him to the table, told him to sit down, and promptly left him alone.

Two Military Police officers stood guard at the front of the tent. His first thought was, *'What about the back? If I wanted to escape, all I have to do is raise the edge of the tent and crawl out. But then I'm done running. Whatever is coming, bring it on.'*

The flap opened, and the men who had escorted him into the tent re-entered. They pulled two chairs up to the opposite side of the table and sat down facing Jake.

"Jake, you need to know that the paperwork is being processed to declare you a deserter, dishonorably discharge you from the army, and charge you with murder, treason, and espionage. We are going to talk with you about those issues here today.

What you say, how you choose to handle this, will dictate where you go from here, but I want you to be clear on this one thing. You are in the custody of the United States government and will be held in a military prison until your case comes to trial.

Your trial will not be public. It will be held in a high-security court to ensure that no further damage to the security of the nation as a result of your actions. Do you understand all of this?" asked the taller of the men.

Jake sat a minute and then said, "I understand that I am in custody. I don't intend to deny my actions, but I'm not sure about the rest of this. Maybe we can start with you telling me your names and what agency you represent."

The two agents looked at each other, and the taller one responded, "You don't need to know our names. When I asked if you understood, I was trying to ascertain if you understood what I said. I was not asking if you understood the reasons or technical aspects of what is before you. Now once more, do you understand what I told you?"

Jake nodded, "Yes, I speak and understand the English language. It is my mother tongue."

"Well, okay. Then the next thing we need to ask is whether or not you intend to cooperate by answering our questions. Is that your intention?"

"Are you going to read me my rights?" Jake asked.

"I am going to break policy and speak frankly. You do not have any rights. You are a traitor. You have carried top secret information, vital to the defense and security of the nation, to our enemies.

You have participated in the killing of two active duty Military Police Criminal Investigation Agents in Fairbanks, and the act of capturing you resulted in the death of a third active duty soldier.

You will soon cease to exist. Your records will be pulled from all of the databases maintained by the defense department and the department of the army. We will lock you away until we feel that you no longer constitute a risk to national security. Your future is one of isolation within our system.

You can, however, make things easier by working with us to identify our weaknesses, to find ways to prevent this from happening again and by helping us understand what information the Soviets were most interested in obtaining from you.

Or, say the word, and we will fly you out of here and lock you up. Which way do you want to go?" the agent asked.

"I am ashamed of my actions. Ask your questions, and I will answer." Jake said.

For the next two hours, the agents had Jake take them through the events leading up to his walking out with the SOP, his relationship with Nikita, the killing of the agents and his flight. They were most interested in his contact with the Soviet Trade Commission in Seattle, and how they arranged for him to leave the country on a plane to Seoul.

Jake told them the whole story, not leaving out or trying to gloss over any detail. He told them about the ambush, the run to the sea and the loss of Johnes. They asked him to repeat the story of the fight on the beach, about him and J.B. keeping the chasers pinned down with the grenades, about his going out to concentrate the smoke on the enemy position and then their flight out.

The taller agent asked the questions, and the shorter one took notes. Jake wondered why they weren't recording the session but figured it was best to answer their questions. *'This sounds like they have already talked with someone about this like they know most of the answers before they ask me the questions,'* Jake thought.

At the end of two hours, the shorter agent stood saying, "I need to take a break. I will be back in a minute."

The taller one said, "Me too. How about you, Jake? Do you need to use the latrine or grab a drink of water?"

Jake said, "No, I don't need to use the latrine. But I am hungry and could use some water."

As the agents turned to leave, one of the Military Police officers raised the flap and stepped in and said, "There is a man out here saying he needs to talk with one of you right now."

The agents kept walking, and the taller one said, "He just hit the jackpot. He gets us both."

Jake was able to see through the opening as the M.P. held the flap back for the agents to exit. He saw another man in civilian clothing pacing back and forth in front of the tent.

The flap dropped, and Jake could hear the three men talking. The flap was lifted, and the three agents came in and sat down. The taller one said, "Jake we have a proposition for you to consider.

We have Nikita in custody. There is some interest in transporting you to the same detention facility and setting the two of you down together for a deeper, more exhaustive debriefing. Depending on how that goes, we might have something else to suggest. What do you think? Will you participate?"

"Yes, I will. Can you tell me where she is?" Jake asked.

The two agents who had been questioning Jake looked at the third one. He shook his head and said, "Our chopper is waiting. They will take you to the next stage." He turned and walked away.

Jake was taken to a jeep, and then to the waiting chopper. The aircraft was unmarked and painted a dull blue.

Fifteen minutes later he was airborne, sitting between the two agents in the bay of the chopper. Ninety minutes later they landed in Nome.

He was loaded onto a small single-engine aircraft marked with the letters NSA. His next stop was Fairbanks. There he was loaded onto a similarly marked jet.

Fatigue overcame hunger, and Jake was soon sleeping. He woke as the jet touched down. Two hours later, he entered the federal detention center at Cheyenne Mountain.

Chapter 18

The Re-Union

Jake was taken to a cell that he thought could be termed Spartan at best. He had barely settled on the metal-framed bunk when the door swung open, and two Air Force Security Police Officers stepped inside his cell. Jake stood, turned his back to them, dropped to his knees, and placed his hands together on the back of his head as he had been instructed to do during the in-processing.

Jake heard, "I am Officer Williams, and my partner is Officer Wheat. We are assigned to be your security escort anytime you are removed from your cell. You will not be allowed to leave the cell when we are not available to escort you. Do not expect, nor ask, to be let out of your cell except in our custody. Is that easy enough for you to grasp?

We are here now to escort you to an interview with federal agents. We are going to start soft. That means handcuffs only. But if you give us any trouble, we will take you down and place you in leg shackles and restraint belt.

My intention is not to threaten or frighten you but understand this, we will hurt you if the need presents itself. Don't doubt me in that."

Handcuffs were snapped on his wrists, and the officers took him by the arms and lifted him to his feet. They turned him to face the door and guided him through it and into the hall.

With one officer holding onto either elbow, they walked him to the closed door of a room where a man in civilian clothing stood in the hallway waiting for his arrival.

"Jake, I am Special Agent Mayfield with the FBI. I am assigned to the Bureau's Counter Intelligence Section. Nikita and some other agents of the government are inside the room behind me. She does not know you are here, but we have talked with her extensively about you. She has been quite open and forthcoming about the interaction between the two of you. She has said some rather nasty things about you, but there seems to be some admiration, and surprise about how you were able to overcome her and Demetrio after she had killed Norwood and Dikes.

We don't know how she is going to react to your presence, but we believe it will be impacted by how you behave toward her. We are interested in is getting every bit of information we can out of her, and in checking the possibility of converting her to a double agent.

We call it flipping, and we know that such a possibility will be greatly enhanced if she is partnered with someone she knows, like you. Do you follow where we are going with this, and are you willing to explore it?"

Jake laughed softly, "Hell yes."

"That's great. We need you to be cool. Don't be too anxious. Just sit and let this play itself out. It might be best to let her take the lead, and you come along like you are willing to do anything to help your situation," Mayfield said. Jake nodded his head in agreement.

Mayfield signaled the officers, and the doors swung open. Nikita turned to see who was entering the room. Her mouth fell open, and she started to stand. Officer Tallifore pushed her back into the chair.

Mayfield pointed Jake to a chair, opposite Nikita. The officers removed his handcuffs and pushed him into the chair.

Jake lifted his eyes and looked across the table at Nikita. Her mouth was still open, and her face reflected utter surprise. "Jake," she said.

"Do you know who this man is, Nikita?" Mayfield asked her.

Without taking her focus from Jake, Nikita said, "You know I do. This is Jake Tolbert. The man we have been talking about."

'I was right, they have been talking about me, and they did know the answers before they asked the questions,' Jake thought to himself.

"Is this the man who you and Demetrio were working for information about the Nike Hercules? Is it true that Demetrio was hidden in the closet and filmed your intimacy? And is it also true that you had planned to use that film to threaten Jake with exposure if he did not give you the information you wanted?" Box asked.

"Yes, all of that is true. Demetrio also photographed and made impressions of his dog tags and identification card while he slept.

We were going to tell him that we would reproduce the identification, place it in a gay bar in Fairbanks and arrange for it to be found by the CID.

Jake, did you know that Demetrio is dead, that you killed him?"

"I didn't mean to kill him. I was trying to get away from the two of you. I'm sorry your friend is dead. So many have died because of me," Jake answered.

Mayfield interrupted their conversation, "Maybe you can talk later, but for now, we need to ask some questions.

Nikita, is it true that your network of agents did background work to identify Jake's family, and were you going to threaten him with showing pictures of the two of you in bed to his minister father and the supervisors of his religious order?"

Nikita nodded yes, then said, "Either that or use the identification planted in the gay bar to make him look like a gay man or at least one who, how do you say, swings both ways. We had not decided, but it made no difference because we never got to that point."

"Why not?" this came from Sorrensby.

"Because the next time Jake showed up at my room, he had a backpack that contained what Demetrio termed the jackpot.

I asked Demetrio what he meant, and he said that Jake had brought the manual outlining the instructions for his position at the Nike Hercules site. Demetrio said it had all the information we would ever need," Nikita said.

"Did you decide to kill Jake, take the manual, and flee the country with it?" Box asked.

"No, we were not going to kill Jake. Demetrio said that by leaving Jake alive, we would be ensuring that our identities would be so well known in the West that our managers would never again assign us outside of the Soviet Union. We saw it as our guarantee of home assignments from that point on. No more field work," Nikita said.

"Nikita, look at me," Sorrensby said. She turned to face the agent.

"Was Jake in the room, and did he participate in the killing of Norwood and Dikes?"

Nikita was shaking her head before Sorrensby finished his question. "Yes, he was in the room, but no he did not participate in the killing. Neither did Demetrio. That was me and me alone."

"You have told us how you killed them, but I want to hear once more what role Jake played in the whole event," Sorrensby said.

"After I killed Dikes, Demetrio told me to search his pockets for the handcuff key. While I was doing that, the other one, Norwood, came back to the room. He knocked on the door. Demetrio stood to open the door, and I stood to the side with the pistol so I could shoot him as he entered the room.

As Demetrio started to open the door, Jake yelled out a warning to Norwood that I had a gun. But it was too late because as soon as the door was unlocked, Norwood pushed it open and came inside the room. I shot him in the face."

"Is that when Jake attacked you," Mayfield asked.

"No, not during the actual shooting. After I shot Norwood, I grabbed his coat to keep him from falling backward and blocking the door. He fell forward, into the room, and I placed the pistol to his head and fired the final round.

I started to go through his pocket looking for the handcuff key, and Jake jumped from the chair and knocked me over. The force of his blow caused me to lose my breath for a minute. Jake grabbed a lamp and struck Demetrio in the face with it. He then removed the key from Norwood's pocket, opened my handcuffs, and locked them onto the ones on Demetrio. We were locked together and helpless.

Jake flushed the handcuff keys, gathered his manual, and left the room. That is the last I saw of him until now," Nikita finished and looked at Jake.

"Are you telling us that while Jake did not try to help Dikes, he did intervene and shouted a warning to Norwood?" Sorrensby pushed for clarification.

"Yes, that's right. But in truth, he didn't have time to warn Dikes. I went into the bathroom to relieve myself, or so he and Dikes thought, and shot Dikes when he opened the door to check on me. They did not know that I had a gun hidden in there." Nikita answered.

"How do you feel about Jake?" Mayfield asked.

"I don't know," Nikita said as she looked long and hard at him.

"I thought he was weak. But the way he acted in that room, charging into me, then hitting Demetrio and what you have told me about his defecting makes me think maybe he is not as weak as I thought.

I do know this, to have escaped from my countrymen, and his certain fate at their hand, to be sitting here now alive and unharmed tells me that he has been through something that no weak man could survive," Nikita said as her voice trailed off.

"Well, Jake. What do you think about what Nikita has said?" Sorrensby asked.

Jake stared at Nikita as he said, "It's all true. Except that I did suspect that she was up to something when she kept pushing Dikes to let her go to the restroom.

I was suspicious when she shamed him into letting her close the door while she did her business. I knew that she was planning something, but I didn't say anything. If I had, maybe Dikes, Norwood, Johnes and all those men we killed on Diomede would still be alive. I wish I could go back and do things differently."

"What do you think about her plan to blackmail you?" Box asked.

Jake smiled, "Now, it doesn't bother me at all. Then, it would have freaked me out."

"Nikita," Sorrensby said, "Jake has told us about how he called the Soviet Trade Mission and that they helped him defect, even gave him a fake passport and helped him through customs and immigration in Seoul. Does this surprise you?"

Nikita said, "Please, Mr. Sorrensby. You know better than that. Every Soviet office in the U.S. has as their first priority the gathering of intelligence to help defeat your nation.

We laugh at your government making it so easy. And if you think the Soviet Union is harvesting information, you should take a look at what the Chinese are doing with their cyber forces. They are even spying on us, our operations here in the U.S."

"Jake, I asked Nikita how she feels about you, and you heard her answer. Now I want to know how you feel about her," Sorrensby asked.

"Well, I have mixed feelings. I mean I was madly in love with her; but at

166

that point, I was the weakling from Iowa Park.

You know, when I was a kid my dad had a guest speaker at our church one summer. That man said something that I had forgotten until I realized what a mistake I had made by running. He said, *'Being a male is a matter of birth. Being a man is a matter of choice. The first step from maleness to manhood is the acceptance of responsibility for and the consequences of one's actions.'*

I found my manhood out there in that frozen Siberian forest, as we ran for the sea and then on the beach where I became an American soldier again. I accept that what I have done is wrong. I am ready to pay the price for my actions.

I said all that to say this, the affection I had for Nikita in Fairbanks is dead because it was the affection of one who no longer exists, for a woman who no longer exists. Now sitting here before her, as a new man, I find myself admiring the courage it takes for her to be so forthright in accepting the responsibility for her actions. I think maybe my answer to you is this, I find her to be a strong woman that I would like to get to know better."

Box nodded and looked at Sorrensby. "I think that covers it for us. The ball is now in your court."

"Not really," Sorrensby said. "I am going to be her handler, but Nikita has to express her mind here. What do you have to say, Nikita?"

Nikita chewed her lower lip, squirmed around in her chair until she was facing Sorrensby. " Well, first of all. I am not an animal that needs a handler. I am a professional who might be managed, but never handled.

Secondly, if you are suggesting what I think you are, I am shocked. I can't believe you would suggest that we could work together outside this facility as an espionage team. You know full well that neither of us would live long outside these walls, and we may not live that long in here."

Sorrensby seemed to be surprised. He arched his eyebrows and said, "I follow that you think the Soviets would hit you on the outside. But first, they would have to know where you were, and then they would have to be able to break the new identification we will give you. We have even talked about some cosmetic surgery for each of you.

We would provide you with new faces, new names, and all the supporting documents to establish and verify your identities. We would install you in new jobs and would be careful to move you from time to time. You would be

167

safe, or as safe as anyone in our business can ever expect."

Nikita leaned forward looking at each of the agents in turn. "During my training, the instructors told us how naïve you Americans are, but I didn't believe it could be so. Now I am seeing it illustrated by men from the highest levels of the American Intelligence and Security Agencies sitting here before me.

Do you not know that we have infiltrated every facet of your society? Our agents teach in and manage your schools, from kindergarten to your graduate and professional programs. We are re-writing your history and teaching our version to your youngest generations.

We preach from your pulpits, conduct your financial affairs from Wall Street to the local bank, announce your news with our twist on it, fight your fires, protect your streets, operate your jails, and serve in every branch of your armed services.

For years we have run our candidates for public office from city hall to Capitol Hill and you Americans elect us over and over.

We control the oval office. Do you believe the occupant of that office to be the most powerful individual on earth? We manage that office from the Kremlin, through the congressmen, the senators, and the appointed officials that our influence and money get elected and placed in office. By the way, that includes your federal judiciary," Nikita looked at the agents realizing the impact she was having on them.

Then she continued, "Mr. Sorrensby, my former bosses will soon know where Jake and I are. We reach so far into your affairs that they will know who does this cosmetic surgery and have pictures of our new faces complete with address and phone numbers before we walk out of the hospital or occupy our new homes.

I can promise you that we have agents within this Cheyenne Mountain you are so proud of. I would not be surprised to find that one of you in this room is one of ours.

Now, do you expect me to willingly walk outside of these walls and make it that much easier for them to kill me? No thank you, sir.

If they do hit me in here, at least there is some chance it will be captured on one of the security cameras you have up and down the halls and hidden in the rooms.

It gives me a degree of comfort to think that the one who kills me stands a better than even chance of being identified and held accountable. No thank you again. I will tough it out here."

Nikita's exposition had sucked the air out of the room. The federal agents sat stunned.

Agent Mayfield found his voice first. "Listen to me, Nikita. It is important that you understand our plan, what we are suggesting is that you and Jake become double agents appearing to work for the Soviets but controlled by us. And yes, we want to have you two operate together, as a team.

If you don't want to do that, all you have to say is no. It is obvious that to be successful as a team, you both would have to be onboard with the plan. We have no plan to force you into this. But now I've got to ask, are you being over dramatic to get out of this, or is there a possibility that you believe all you have said?"

"What I said is true. I am not being over dramatic. Secondly, I have no objection to being with Jake. I too would like to start over and establish a relationship with this new man before me. But I do not want to die, and that is precisely what will happen, how you say sooner than later, if you put me outside these walls.

We agreed that I would tell you everything I know in exchange for you keeping me in relative comfort here in as much security as possible. I want you to honor your word to me," Nikita said.

Mayfield looked at Sorrensby and shrugged. "Okay, but let me ask you if there is a possibility that you were told all of this to create so much fear that you would never consider working for us if and when we captured you?"

"Not a chance. They told us straight up that if we were captured and were flipped, that we would be killed, and that our families back home would also be killed. I believe them because they do not bluff," Nikita said.

Sorrensby pushed back from the table and stood. "Well, there it is. She is not going to cooperate. I don't know that I believe we are compromised to the point that she says, but to be safe, I'm going to move her and keep moving her.

Her information is so valuable that I intend to make her as hard a target as possible. If you have any other questions, ask them now because you will not see her after we walk out of this room."

Mayfield shifted his gaze to Box, who shook his head and said, "I got nothing else to ask, boss."

Mayfield stood and extended his hand to Sorrensby. "It was a good idea. I wish we could have put it together. We wish you nothing but the best of luck with her."

Mayfield turned to look at Nikita. "I don't want to believe what you have said here. I hope you are wrong, but I have no ill will toward you. I wish you a long life."

Box stood and said to Officer Williams, "Please take Jake back to his cell."

He leaned over and placed his hand on Jakes' shoulder. "Sorry, it didn't work out Jake. Get a good night's sleep.
We will talk tomorrow. Give us some time to figure our next step out."

Williams said, "Stand up, Jake."

Jake stood, and turned to face Williams, "Can I ask the agents one more thing?"

Officer Wheat said, "Make it quick, our shift is about to end."

Jake looked at Sorrensby and said, "I would appreciate some time, maybe an hour to talk with Nikita, just the two of us, here at this table. I mean what can it hurt, where can we go."

Officer Wheat said, "No way. Williams and I are signed for you, and you do not leave our presence. Say goodbye now because you're headed back to your cell."

Jake leaned over to Nikita. "If you are still here tomorrow, maybe we can eat breakfast together and talk some."

Nikita smiled and said, "I would like that, *Big Spender*."

Wheat and Williams pushed Jake toward the door, out into the hall and to his cell. They put him down on his knees, removed the handcuffs and backed out of his cell.

Jake stayed on his knees until he heard the heavy doors slam closed. Then he rose, walked to his cot and lay down. His last conscious thought before dropping into a deep sleep was of Nikita. He could still smell her fragrance, even though it was nothing more than the prison soap and shampoo. He dreamed about what he was going to say to her at breakfast.

Chapter 19

Paul Revere

After Jake was out of the room, Sorrensby turned to Tallifore, "How long you been in the Air Force, officer?"

"I am halfway through my second hitch. So that makes six years and counting. Why do you ask?" She smiled.

Sorrensby shrugged, "I was just wondering."

"That is a bad habit you have there. Do it enough, and it will become your identity," Tallifore said.

"Take her back to her cell, and be sure someone is watching her around the clock. I am coming for her early, and I expect her to be well and ready to travel," Sorrensby said.

"I'm going off duty too, but I'm sure she will be fine. That is unless one of those secret agents, she told you about, can get to her," Tallifore laughed.

"You think she is wrong about there being Soviet agents inside this facility?" Sorrensby asked.

"I don't believe any of it. Not for a minute. You know the background check we go through to get in here. And it continues as long we are on active duty along with the periodic polygraph tests.

Nothing goes undetected. She might believe it, I certainly don't. Go drink your cold beer, and she will be here for you when you want her," Tallifore said.

Sorrensby looked her over, nodded, and turned to leave. When he reached the door, he paused, looked back and winked at Nikita. "See you early," he said.

Tallifore said, "Let's go, Nikita. I want to get you settled in for the night so that I can go home."

Nikita stood and said, "Is it possible that you could tell the morning

shift to wake Jake and me early so we can have some time at breakfast before the agent comes for me?"

172

Tallifore hesitated, and Nikita said, "Please. He doesn't know it, but I think I might be carrying his child. I want to be able to tell him before I am moved."

Tallifore groaned and rolled her eyes. "Lord, Nikita. How did you let that happen? Never mind. It doesn't matter anyway. Yes, I will see what I can do for you two lovebirds. But only because of the baby."

Nikita walked to her cell thinking about seeing Jake. *'What would he say when she told him that he was going to be a father?'*

Just before they got to her cell, she asked, "Officer Tallifore, could I ask one more favor. Would it be possible for me to get a laxative? I am so constipated that I am starting to cramp."

Nikita knew the rule that only the nurse or a physician could authorize any medication but was hoping Tallifore was feeling tender toward her because of her maternal state. Still, she was surprised when Tallifore readily agreed saying, "Absolutely. I will be right back."

Nikita brushed her teeth, washed her face, and then changed into her sleeping gown. She was about to lie down when the cell door swung open, and Tallifore walked in. She made sure Nikita had eye contact with her then pursed her lips to form the word, *shush*, and slipped a pill into Nikita's hand. Nikita grasped it and turned to the sink and filled her cup with water. She slipped the tablet into the cup and swallowed water and pill.

Nikita smiled at the camera and turned intending to say goodnight to Tallifore. She was surprised that Tallifore was already out of the room and had eased the door closed so quietly that no sound was generated.

'That's strange,' thought Nikita. Her hand went to her throat, *'surely Tallifore is not one of them. No of course not. I am being silly. I will get a good night's sleep, and then have breakfast with Jake. I will tell him about his child I am carrying.'*

Nikita lay down and was soon asleep. The officer on duty noticed that her breathing was not as loud as before and trained the camera around for a close-up view. She saw that Nikita was on her side facing the wall, and figured that was the reason she was not able to hear her breathing. She reset the camera and went back to reading her magazine.

The second watch came on at five. The officer assigned to Nikita, Staff Sergeant Toni Reardon, read the note Tallifore had left and thought, *'what the hell, it can't hurt anything.'*

Sergeant Reardon grabbed the keys and walked down to Nikita's cell. She rattled the keys in the lock and waited for half a second to give Nikita a chance to sit up. Opening the door, she was surprised to see Nikita on her side.

'*She is very still,*' Reardon thought as panic welled up in her. She sprinted across the floor and reached for Nikita's shoulder. She jerked her hand back as she felt the cold flesh of Nikita's upper arm.

Reardon wheeled around, stepped into the hallway and pushed the red panic button. The early morning was shattered as the horns screamed their alert, reverberating into the lobby where Special Agent Sorrensby was entering.

Sorrensby gulped for air. He slid his card through the reader and pulled on the door. It would not open, and the Security Police Officer in the control room opened the speaker to say, "Sorry sir, but we have an alert in here. All entry is prohibited until we get this handled."

"But I'm Special Agent Sorrensby of the National Security Agency. I am here to move a high-security prisoner. You must let me in."

The officer shook his head no, closed the speaker, and walked away.

Forty-five minutes later Sorrensby rose from the bench as the door to the secure area opened. He watched, with gall rising into his throat, as a team of medics rolled a gurney out with a sheet-covered figure strapped on.

"Hold on a minute. I need to see her," Sorrensby said.

"How do you know we have a woman?" one of the medics asked.

Sorrensby replied, "I know because she tried to tell me this was going to happen. And it did. Right here in the most secure military prison we have."

He pulled the sheet back and stared into the face of Nikita.

Sorrensby dropped the sheet and nodded. The medics rolled the gurney out and away down the long hallway.

Sorrensby sat on the bench in the lobby. In a few minutes, Mayfield and Box came in. They took one look at Sorrensby and saw the truth on his face.

Sorrensby stood and said, "They hit her last night. She's dead."

Mayfield asked, "What about Jake?"

"I don't know," Sorrensby said.

"How did they hit her?" Box asked.

Sorrensby just shrugged. *'Such a bad habit,'* he mused.

Wait a minute he thought, *'Nikita had said that to him. Her trainers had told her to avoid habits that would become her identity. Tallifore had said the same thing. Why would Tallifore say that? Who had taught her not to develop habits that identify you? Why would that matter in her position?'*

Mayfield had gone inside to check on Jake while Sorrensby sat in thought.

"Jake is okay," Mayfield said.

"For now," Box said.

"He's right, you know. Best thing to do is take him out of here right now. Let's park him with someone we know we can trust and then let's hustle over to personnel and examine Officer Tallifore's file," Sorrensby said.

"Why do you want to see her personnel file?" Box asked.

"I need to answer a question," Sorrensby said.

A half hour later, the three agents stood in front of Tallifore's apartment door. Sorrensby knocked, and the door opened, yielding under the pressure of his knock.

The agents stepped back, and Sorrensby called out, "Officer Tallifore. It's Agent Sorrensby. I need to talk to you. May we come in?"

There was no answer. They entered the apartment. On the table in the kitchen, they saw a picture of Tallifore in her Air Force Security Police uniform. Lying on the table in front of it was a single sheet of paper.

Sorrensby picked it up and read:

You should have believed Nikita and carried her with you when you left last night.

We reported her arrival at the Cheyenne while she was being processed. My command (no Sorrensby, we do not have handlers because we are human beings, not animals) told me that she was to be eliminated as soon as possible.

I had a kill pill in reserve. I was in a quandary as to how I was going to get it to her, but then she solved my problems by telling me she was constipated and asked for a laxative. I slipped the tablet to her. She dropped it into a cup of water and swallowed it quite willingly.

You will have to wait on the autopsy to find out what it was. I don't know, or I would gladly tell you. Oh, by the way. She is pregnant with Jake's child. We got a two for one. Sorry, don't mean to be crass but we make it a practice to remove all of the bloodlines of a traitor. Jake is next. You know we will get him.

What Nikita told you is true. Do you know what is interesting? There was another Nikita (Khrushchev) who said much the same thing. You dismissed the First Secretary as an ignorant barbarian beating his shoe on a table. But his message was one of prophecy. He said we would bury you and here we are doing so, albeit in small steps.

We could hoist our flag in D.C. today if we wanted. And your vaunted technology and smart weapons could do nothing to stop us. For we are seated in your command structure and we control your weapons systems!

Don't bother trying to find me. I was beyond your reach long before you discovered Nikita's body. That's not to say we won't see each other again someday.

I am intrigued by the thought of taking you into one of our detention centers and watching our agents work with you.

Keep looking behind you. Is that my step you hear, my shadow you see? Can you turn over in your bed and ignore that bump in the night? Hey, here's something you can think on, are you voting for us the next time you cast your ballot?

Your Paul Reverie rode through the night sounding the alarm, "The British are coming." It is much too late for that this time, Agent Sorrensby, for we are already here! And besides that, you Americans are so confident in your invincibility that no one will believe the next Paul Reverie.

Finally, my real name is Tasha Romanoff. I am what you Americans call your worst nightmare. I am a Soviet Warrior, and I am not only re-writing your past but also authoring your future. Accept it and live, or resist us and die.

You can't 'shrug' us off!

Tasha

Sorrensby had stepped onto the patio to read the note. As he finished reading it, Box and Mayfield stepped from the apartment and stood beside him.

"What did she say," Box asked.

"Oh, just a lot of gibberish about how the U.S.S.R. is going to conquer us from within. But she did admit that she is a Soviet agent. She said she reported to her command that Nikita was in Cheyenne. Her orders came down to eliminate Nikita. She poisoned her.

Tallifore, or Tasha as she is named, gave her the tablet. Nikita dropped it in a cup of water and drank it down. Tasha said we would have to wait for the autopsy to find out what the poison was, and she said the autopsy would give us a surprise, Nikita was pregnant with Jake's child.

One last thing you two need to know. She said that her command knew Jake was at Cheyenne and that they would get him. If I were you and wanted to work Jake, I would move him now. I would move him into a safe house with twenty-four seven protection," Sorrensby said.

Mayfield glanced over at Box, then faced Sorrensby and asked, "Jake who?"

"Want to go drink a cold one?" Box asked.

Mayfield nodded and said, "Why not. What are we going to drink to?"

Sorrensby shrugged and said, "How about Paul Revere."

Mayfield said, "Or maybe those warriors who are holding the front line there in Alaska, let's go drink one to those *Arctic Warriors*."

The End

About The Author

Ken Bangs is the author of <u>Arctic Warriors</u>. Ken was a police officer for the City of Dallas, Texas when he was drafted into the United States Army. He was assigned to the Alaska Command where he served as a Military Police Officer.

Ken holds a B.S. in Criminal Justice from Sam Houston State University, a M.S. in Human Relations and Business Management from Amber University and a Doctorate of Ministry in Christian Counseling from Jacksonville Theological Seminary.

Ken has been married to Trudy Turner Bangs for 51 years. They have two children and two 'perfect' grandchildren. They currently live in McKinney, Texas.

The author in uniform shortly before he
was drafted into the United States Army.

The author Officer assigned the 562nd

Patch worn by members of the United States Armed Forces Alaskan Command

Shoulder patch worn by soldiers assigned to the United States Army Alaska (USARAL)

This is an example of the fire control scope operated by Jake in *Arctic Warriors.*

Note the squib test log on the shelf, in front of the scope. The MPs referred to the soldiers who worked the scopes as scope dopes.

Nike Hercules (initially designated SAM-A-25, and later MIM-14) was a solid fuel-propelled two-stage surface-to-air missile used by U.S. and NATO armed forces for medium and high-altitude long-range air defense.

It could also be employed in a surface-to-surface role (like a standard artillery piece or cannon), and had a demonstrated ability to hit other short-range missiles. The Nike Hercules could carry either a nuclear warhead or a conventional high explosive warhead (T-45 fragmentation type).

The missile had a range of about 77 miles (124 km) and traveled at Mach 3.65 or 2,750 miles an hour. These are shown in the firing position on rails but they were also stored underground in and fired form silos called pits. The soldiers working in the pits were referred to as "pit rats."
e positions as "Scope Dopes."

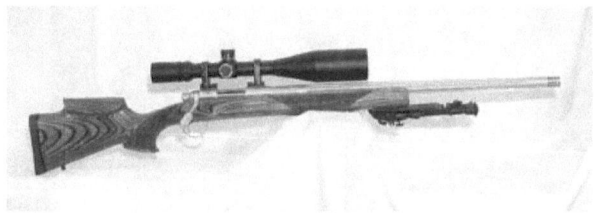

The Specialized 7.62 rifle carried by Johnes "The Shooter" in *Arctic Warriors*. Johnes was detailed to concentrate his fire on specified targets at long range. The scope, bolt action and folding rest provided more accuracy at long distance. With the bolt-action rifle, Johnes had to work the action to eject shell casing and load a new round after each shot. This meant he had limited ability to engage in a rapid-fire exchange with the enemy.

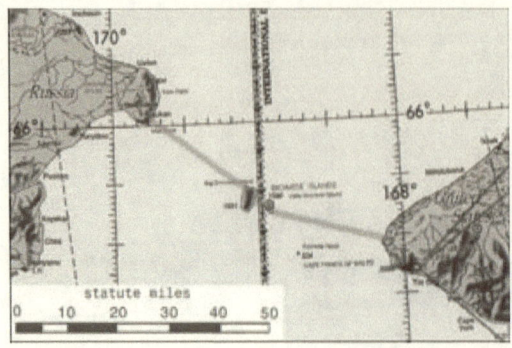

Illustration of the Diomede Islands, Big Diomede belonging to the USSR and Little Diomede to the United States. Note how close they are, separated by 2.4 miles of water at their closest point.

In the novel *Arctic Warriors*, the Texans lifted off from Little Diomede, swinging southwest before turning back North to sit down on an LZ (landing zone) 4 Klicks (Kilometers or 2 miles) inland of the beach.

Following the ambush, they had to run south and west through a Siberian Blizzard to the tip of Big Diomede, where they would connect with the helicopters that would extract them.

Note the flight path of the extraction. They flew over Little Diomede to land at Base Camp Redstone, located in the center of the Bering Land Bridge National Preserve, some 120 miles after going 'feet dry' by crossing the cost of Alaska at Nome.

Other Books By Ken Bangs

Rosco Jack of Gateway Farm

Guardians In Blue

Guardians In Blue: Book Two

The Adventurous Travels of Miranda and J-Dog

Out of Saul ~ Paul
"From Tarsus to *Aquae Salviae*"

Daniel, Historian, and Prophet

Moses ~ Prince of Egypt, son of Abraham

Securing Your Church ~ Keeping it Safe: a Planning Guide

The Levee

Killing Joe Redfern

Morning Dew

www.ingramcontent.com/pod-product-compliance
Lightning Source LLC
Chambersburg PA
CBHW032009170626
46807CB00006B/2718